"This is crazy, ~~Gunn.~~
You can't just crash in there."

"But you can?" He found his jacket and turned to Hannah, holding it out so she could help him into it. She responded automatically, and he stiffened his arms as she put the coat on him, the protector hard against his spine, a trickle of sweat already rolling down his back.

She buckled him in, and he saw that her hands were trembling.

"We haven't done enough recon yet...."

"Hannah! We don't have time for that." He plucked his helmet from the rear of the SUV and thrust it on his head. "We have to get those kids out first. Then we'll deal with the bomb."

"No," she said, almost in a whisper. "This is wrong. All wrong..."

He stared at her in puzzled surprise. Her face was flushed and her blue eyes were glowing with alarm. She was the least prone to gut feelings. Why this? Why now?

He reached out and tucked a stand of hair behind her ear, the silk curl soft and fragrant. "Everything will be fine. We've got a date tonight, remember? I wouldn't do anything to mess that up." He bent and kissed her, the taste of her lips lingering on his own. Then he ran toward the building.

He was barely over the threshold when the bomb detonated.

Dear Reader,

After September 11, 2001, the people of America, including me, began to understand and appreciate many aspects of our lives that we had previously taken for granted. The heroics of the police, firefighters and rescue personnel who responded so selflessly to that tragedy moved to the top of my list of "things I won't forget." I simply cannot imagine the courage it would take to race *toward* a horrible disaster that everyone else is fleeing. Think about that…. Could you risk your life for a group of total strangers?

I don't believe I could, but on that day, hundreds of men and women did that very thing. And many more do it *every* day.

From the cop who stops a speeder to the soldier guarding a foreign hill, there are people whose job it is to keep us safe. We can worship as we like, live as we prefer, travel where we want because of these incredibly brave individuals.

The men and women in *The Target*, the fourth book in my series THE GUARDIANS, are representative of these people. Quinn McNichol and Hannah Crosby are members of a national bomb squad. Both are prepared to give their lives for strangers, but neither is happy about the other doing the same.

Nothing I can write comes close to explaining the experiences of the men and women who make up our bomb squads. Tomorrow morning when you walk into the grocery store for a loaf of bread or into the drugstore to pick up some cough syrup, take a moment to think about what you *aren't* feeling. You aren't scared that the trash can by the door might blow up. You aren't anxiously thinking that the car pulling in next to yours might explode. You don't give a second thought to the package the woman ahead of you in line accidentally leaves behind.

You feel safe and secure because you know the men and women of our law enforcement agencies are on the job, ready to give their lives for you. Next time you see one, express how much you appreciate him or her.

Sincerely,

Kay David

The Target
Kay David

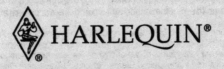

HARLEQUIN®

TORONTO • NEW YORK • LONDON
AMSTERDAM • PARIS • SYDNEY • HAMBURG
STOCKHOLM • ATHENS • TOKYO • MILAN • MADRID
PRAGUE • WARSAW • BUDAPEST • AUCKLAND

ISBN 0-373-71131-X

THE TARGET

Visit us at www.eHarlequin.com

Printed in U.S.A.

I'd like to take this opportunity to acknowledge some
very special people: Dr. Lynch, Dr. Ripepi, Dr. King and
the "real" Dr. Barroso. All of you will forever have a special
place in my heart because of your dedication and kindness,
which no words can possibly describe.

To Rhonda Whitton, Pat Herendon and Debra Fyles, my
deepest gratitude for your continued understanding and
help.

And finally to Reba. Your love and support mean more to
me than I can say. Thank you for everything.

Books by Kay David

HARLEQUIN SUPERROMANCE

798—THE ENDS OF THE EARTH
823—ARE YOU MY MOMMY?
848—THE MAN FROM HIGH MOUNTAIN
888—TWO SISTERS
945—OBSESSION
960—THE NEGOTIATOR*
972—THE COMMANDER*
985—THE LISTENER*
1045—MARRIAGE TO A STRANGER
1074—DISAPPEAR

Coming soon: THE SEARCHERS—Harlequin Superromance #1149
   (Available August 2003)

*Books in THE GUARDIANS series

Don't miss any of our special offers. Write to us at the
following address for information on our newest releases.

Harlequin Reader Service
U.S.: 3010 Walden Ave., P.O. Box 1325, Buffalo, NY 14269
Canadian: P.O. Box 609, Fort Erie, Ont. L2A 5X3

Prologue

HANNAH CROSBY LIFTED her head from the pillow and stared at the man beside her. After their lovemaking, he'd dropped into a light sleep, his chest rising and falling with a rhythm that matched the lengthening afternoon shadows. They'd been in the tangled sheets for almost two hours, and the rays now dipped low enough to bypass the blinds and raise the temperature of the bedroom. The overhead fan did little to help, but then again, Hannah wasn't sure anything could cool the heated blood that still coursed through her body.

Quinn McNichol had that kind of effect on her.

How did he do it? What secret did he know? Where had he learned to make her feel the way he did?

She'd pondered these questions for more than two and a half years—since the day, in fact, that she'd joined the federal bomb squad he'd already belonged to. A firefighter for several years before that point, Hannah had wanted to become a member of EXIT—the Explosives and Incendiary Team—for a long time, but what she remembered most about her first day at work was meeting Quinn, a senior tech in the New Orleans group. She could still recall shaking his hand that morning. His strong grip had set up a chain reaction inside her body unlike anything she'd ever felt before.

And it was still going on.

Sometimes he managed it with just a look. Sometimes he did it with a kiss. Usually, it was just a simple touch—his finger against her cheek, his hand on her arm, his mouth on her neck. Whatever it was, the result was always the same: she would lose control. Another woman would take over Hannah's body and do things with it that the normal Hannah would never consider. Quinn unleashed something in her that no one else had ever been able to even find, much less set free. She'd throw herself into his arms and within seconds, their clothes would be gone. They'd made love in so many strange places, she'd lost count.

She edged closer to him, the scent from their bodies lingering between them. Quinn was a tall, striking man, his skin bronzed from the time they spent outside, the richness of the color spiced by his Cajun blood. His dark hair and even darker eyes garnered looks from women everywhere they went, no matter the circumstances. His looks alone couldn't explain his effect on her, though. She'd been around good-looking, macho men her entire career, from firefighters to cops. None of them had made her crazy.

Maybe it couldn't be explained, she thought suddenly. Maybe it was simply magic. She looked at him a moment longer, then rolled to her back and sighed in frustration. Why did it matter what she called it? He had it and she fell for it. Every time.

Otherwise, she would have left him long ago.

The bed moved and she felt his gaze on her profile. He was a light sleeper—they both were, a habit born from years of dangerous work.

"What are you thinking about?" He reached out for a strand of her hair and twisted it around his finger. His question was rhetorical because he could read her mind as well as her body.

Her eyes met his and she felt their intensity all the way down to the bottom of her feet. "You."

He grinned lazily and another zing shot through her. Using the tip of the curl he'd made, he brushed the ends of her hair over the tops of her breasts. "That's good," he said. "I like it when you think about me."

"You do?" She turned to face him, their lips now inches apart. "Why is that?"

"It makes me think you love me."

"You *know* I love you."

"That's true, but a little reinforcement goes a

long way. Everyone likes to know they're on the right track.''

She feathered her fingers over his stubbled jaw. The words she wanted to say would spoil this moment between them, but Hannah couldn't stop herself.

''You're right,'' she agreed slowly. ''Everyone likes to know that, including me.''

Their eyes locked and his gaze hardened, his voice becoming deceptively soft as he warned her. ''We've had a really great day, Hannah. Don't do this…''

She shook her head, her hair whispering against the pillows. ''I have to, Quinn. It's too important to me—to us—not to talk about it.''

He sat up and swung his feet to the floor. ''But it's *all* we talk about.'' The muscles in his back tensed and rippled tightly. He stayed silent for a moment, then he twisted around to look at her. His jaw was a single line of anger, his lips pursed tightly. ''How many times do we have to go over this, Hannah? It just isn't possible right now….''

In the quiet that followed, she could hear the excited cries of the kids down the street. There was an empty lot on the corner, and the evening stillness often rang with the noise the neighborhood children raised as they played tag and red rover and whatever else they could dream up. Hannah loved to listen to them, but right now, the sound was almost painful.

"It isn't possible only because of you. I won't see thirty-two again and time is passing. I want a family. I want a husband. I want—"

He stood abruptly and stalked to the window. "I know what you want, Hannah. Believe me, I know."

With a catch in her throat, Hannah sat up and pulled the sheet around her. Because her own childhood had been just the opposite, she'd always wanted a houseful of children and a special place to call home. Her father's job had demanded constant travel. He'd never been home. Her mother, Barbara, had finally divorced him, saying he was never there, anyway, so why should they stay together?

The answer had become quickly apparent. Without his income, Barbara had had to return to work to support the two of them. They'd sold the home where Hannah had grown up and moved into an apartment on the other side of town. Hannah and her mother became even closer in their adversity— and were still—but with no siblings and none of her friends nearby, Hannah had ended up spending more time than ever alone and she'd been miserable and lonely.

To compensate, she'd made up another family for herself, complete with a set of twins and three other brothers, a mother who stayed home and baked cookies and a father who went to work at eight and came home at five. It'd been a fantasy, but it'd sustained her for a long time, even leading her, she was now convinced, to her earlier career as a firefighter. Living in the firehouse with all the other firefighters had made her feel like part of a huge family and she'd loved it. Until she'd heard about EXIT. Nothing less than the excitement that assignment had promised could have taken her away from her substitute brothers.

She took a deep breath and continued the running argument. "Then if you know what I want, when are we going to do something about it?"

"People who have children have to be responsible for them." He faced her. "As long as we do what we do, I'm not going to bring a child into this world. It's too risky."

Grabbing the sheet, Hannah rose to her knees and shook her head. "I disagree! And even if that was true, I've told you—"

"I know what you've told me—you'd quit. But a kid needs two parents, a mother *and* a father—"

"I'm well aware of what—"

"No, you aren't aware of anything or you wouldn't be asking for the kind of commitment you are. It's not fair. To me or to the poor kid we'd leave behind if one of us got blown to hell and back!"

This certainly wasn't the first time she'd heard

Quinn say something so harsh, but for some reason, the words cut deeper than usual. Hannah stayed where she was a second longer, then she got out of the bed. Her legs were shaking with anger, but she remained silent. If she spoke right now, she'd say something she'd regret later.

Quinn crossed the room, reaching for her. Knowing it was pointless, but trying anyway, she ducked his embrace. He took another step and captured her, his hands on her bare shoulders, his eyes cajoling as he stared down at her.

"You know I'm telling you the truth." He moved his fingers as he spoke, his thumb rubbing her collarbone, his other fingers massaging her shoulders. Hannah fought to ignore the sensation he was creating.

"I know you're telling me what you *think* is the truth," she said. "But you're wrong, Quinn. Very, very wrong. Our jobs are only dangerous if someone screws up."

"Which *does* happen."

"But not often."

"It only takes once."

"Then we'll both quit."

A tense moment passed, then he bent his head and kissed her, the feel of his mouth blanking out everything else. She swayed in his embrace, but he held her tight. When the kiss was over, he raised his head and looked at her, his breath soft on her cheeks. "I'm not going to quit. And neither are you."

"But—"

"That's not the answer to this problem. You'd resent the sacrifice every day for the rest of your life. You'd end up hating yourself...and me."

She tried to think of a counter to his logic, but thinking was impossible with his body pressed to hers and his hands stroking her back.

"You have to be responsible for the children you bring into this world, Hannah. Kids can't raise themselves, and when they try, they get piss-poor results."

Hannah had always thought she could change Quinn's mind—she'd changed everything else in her life she didn't like—but she was beginning to despair. With dogged determination, she tried one more time.

"But we'll be here," she said. "We'll raise them ourselves. We can be responsible for them—"

"Hush, Hannah, hush..." he murmured, bending down to nuzzle her neck. "We don't need kids at this point in our lives. Maybe sometime in the distant future—but not just yet. I can be enough for you now if you'll let me—"

"But, Quinn—"

He cut off her protest with a kiss, pulling her down with him to the bed they'd just abandoned.

She cursed herself and her weakness, then she gave in—once more—and closed her eyes. Quinn's magical touch banished the argument from her mind.

But not from her heart.

CHAPTER ONE

Three months later—January

"YOU STILL HAVE THAT little black dress hanging in the back of the closet?"

Quinn paused beside Hannah's desk and she looked up at him. Her eyes were a startling shade of light blue. Sometimes when they were in bed, they almost looked translucent, but right now, as she glared at him, they went dark with suspicion. They'd had another "discussion" about a family the night before and she was still angry. But he hadn't budged and he wouldn't. He'd been around a lot longer than Hannah, and he knew their profession much better than she did.

In the flash and heat of a single second, he'd seen friends—people he cared about—disappear in a pink cloud. She didn't understand, and frankly, he hoped she never would. The knowledge was costly, to your body and your soul.

"I think it's in there somewhere," Hannah answered. "Why are you asking?"

"I want you to wear it tonight." He forced aside his grim thoughts and concentrated on the present. "We're going to Galatoire's."

The name of her favorite restaurant brought an involuntary smile, but then her lips tightened. "If you think taking me somewhere fancy is going to make things okay, you can forget about it. Crab cakes and deviled oysters won't do the trick this time, Quinn." She shook her head. "And I mean it."

She'd said these words last night and he'd heard them before, as well, but a new resolve seemed to be growing behind them. Someone else might not have noticed, but Quinn had picked up on it instantly.

Sometimes he hated his instincts.

Life would be much simpler for him if he was more like Hannah. She didn't intuit things or emotions—if it wasn't before her in black and white, it simply didn't exist. Everything had hidden nuances for Quinn; he could read the tension in a room by simply walking into it. Hannah's way was better. What she didn't know, she didn't worry about. What she didn't accept, she changed.

Until she'd hooked up with him.

He leaned close enough to smell her shampoo and see the freckle on her right cheek that she always tried to hide with makeup. Being this near was all it took to make him want her. His concern over their fight evaporated.

"This is more than just dinner. A lot more."

She arched one blond eyebrow. "Like what?"

"It's a surprise."

"I don't like surprises," Hannah said flatly. "And I think we need to talk about last night. I'm not going to let this drop, Quinn—"

"No talking." He stopped her words with a light kiss and shook his head, saying, "Tonight. Dinner." Then he walked away, his surprise intact.

He'd given the evening ahead a lot of thought. When Quinn told Hannah his news, he wanted to do it right, not blurt it out in the middle of the bullpen. Bill Ford, their boss, had told Quinn that morning he'd been selected to be the new team lead. Bill was moving on to Washington. The announcement would be made next week, but for the moment, no one knew about the promotion except Quinn. And Bobby Justice.

Quinn made his way down the hall to his office, the tall, black tech on his mind. Bobby had been the only other serious candidate for the job. Well-respected and just as competent as Quinn, Bobby had been on the team even longer, fourteen years to Quinn's twelve. He was a quiet, steady man whose life revolved around his wife and children, but he—

and everyone else on the team—lacked the one essential Quinn had in abundance.

He had a mysterious, indefinable touch. However much he downplayed the ability when others mentioned it, Quinn couldn't deny the truth to himself; he had a sixth sense about bombs. The others on the team were all terrific, especially Hannah, whose strength was analysis. But Quinn's skill was unique. Consequently no one really understood it. Including him.

He reached his office, stepped inside and went to work. The mundane details always piled up—reports to read and file, examinations to be studied, fragments to examine... This was his least favorite part of the job and he tended to put it off. That technique might have worked in the past, but as the boss, he'd have to be better at dealing with it all. He worked steadily until noon, then stopped for lunch.

The call came in right after one.

Bobby appeared at Quinn's door, every line in his face drawn with worry. "There's a problem off the Central Business District," he said. "CBD dispatch caught a suspicious package and sent out a coupla uniforms. It looks bad."

"They all look bad," Quinn said.

"Not like this. It could be Mr. Rogers...." Bobby paused. "That's why they called and gave us a heads-up."

"Oh, man…are you sure?"

"The box is propped up against the back door of a day-care center, adjacent to a school. Kids everywhere. Metro's dogs alerted on it…all the pieces are in place…"

At Bobby's words Quinn felt his stomach roll over. EXIT had been tracking a serial bomber for what felt like ten lifetimes. They'd linked him to three bombings across the South, each occurring every two years for the past six; one in Georgia, one in Mississippi and one in South Carolina. Day-care centers in run-down neighborhoods were his targets, hence the "Mr. Rogers" nickname. The team had been on edge for the whole month. The bomber didn't always strike on the exact same day, but the month—January—never changed. His devices were frighteningly potent, and it'd been a miracle that no one had been killed. Yet.

Hannah came up behind Bobby. She already had on the black leather jacket they wore when they were called out, with EXIT embroidered across the back in bright yellow letters. Right behind her was Mark Baker, the newest member of the team. Baker grated on everyone's nerves, making up for his lack of experience with bluster. Without conscious effort, at least on Quinn's part, a rivalry seemed to be developing between the two of them.

Bobby ignored the other techs and focused on

Quinn. "I'm going over there. If it's him, we need to know. I can take a quick look, then tell the rest of you what's up with it."

Quinn understood the reaction—he'd like to do the same, but he held up his hand. "Hold on. Did Central request our help? I thought you said it was just a heads-up call."

A federal agency, EXIT primarily dealt with two situations: explosions at government facilities or cases that proved to be unusual in some way, such as the serial bomber. With five offices nationwide, they only went to local sites as a courtesy, and even then, their expertise had to be formally requested.

"Well, it was but—"

"Then it's their baby until they want to give it up." Quinn spoke calmly, sending Bobby a look that only the two of them understood. Before now they'd worked by loose consensus, Ford more intent on getting to Washington than forging a team. Quinn wanted something different. "Let's wait. I don't want to piss off the guys over there—"

Hannah spoke up, disregarding them all. "We've never had a potential site this fresh. I'm going now." Interagency rivalries were meaningless to her. She only wanted to get the job done. She zipped her jacket, then looked at the men expectantly. "Who's coming with me?"

Baker spoke instantly. "I'm ready."

Bobby hesitated. He obviously wanted to go, but he just as clearly didn't want to upset Quinn.

Hannah headed for the door, then paused at the threshold. "You in or out, Bobby?"

The big man sent Quinn an apologetic look and shrugged. "She's goin', I'm goin'."

Quinn cursed, then he jumped up from his desk and grabbed his own jacket. *What the hell,* he thought. *Monday I'll be a big-shot manager. I'll make this call and it'll be my last one.*

He had no idea how right he was.

FIVE MINUTES LATER, striding through the parking lot of EXIT's headquarters, Hannah asked herself the question that had plagued her ever since she'd joined the team.

What kind of sicko would leave a bomb at a day-care center?

The very idea made her want to simultaneously throw up and shoot someone. They were just little kids, for God's sake! How could anyone be so twisted, so evil? And now it'd happened here in New Orleans, right under their noses. The fact that one day she might have to put her own children in a facility like the one they were headed for made the whole situation even more difficult for Hannah.

If she ever had any children of her own...

Quinn jumped behind the wheel of the response vehicle, and Hannah climbed in the back with Mark, leaving Bobby to go up front. She didn't want to be any closer to Quinn than she had to be. At the moment, he *also* made her feel like throwing up and shooting someone, preferably him.

Their fight still stung. Why in the hell couldn't he commit? She was too damn old for the hot-and-cold, up-and-down, crazy connection they shared. They'd argue, then he'd charm his way back into her good graces. A month or so later, they'd repeat the cycle. Their romance was becoming as unstable and erratic as the bombs they encountered, and she was getting tired of it. The only constant between them—their lovemaking—had yet to suffer, but that was part of the problem, wasn't it? When Quinn touched her, Hannah put everything else aside, including, she'd determined lately, her brain.

Buckling her seat belt, she recalled the previous night's argument. It'd been the same as always: she wanted kids, Quinn didn't. He'd used the old excuse of their jobs, but other techs had families—look at Bobby.

It was time to make a decision.

And this time, she actually meant it. She'd had her fill. She wouldn't succumb to Quinn's lingering kisses and slow hands anymore. After dinner tonight, she'd tell him exactly what she wanted and if he couldn't—or wouldn't—change, then she had to move on. They'd been together two years and she

loved Quinn so much it frightened her, but she refused to continue this way. She wanted a husband,
a home and children.

The decision to abandon the relationship made her
world sway. All at once, she remembered something
Quinn had told her…how when a bomb exploded,
the universe shifted, and things were never the same
again. Ever.

She usually didn't get Quinn's mystical pro-
nouncements and this one had been no different, but
she suddenly understood. Turning as if to stare out
the window, she blinked rapidly and told herself she
was doing the right thing. She had no other choice
if she wanted to keep her self-respect and have the
family she'd always dreamed about. After a few
painful seconds, she forced everything to the back
of her mind—she *had* to concentrate on the moment.
Nothing could take away her focus from what was
ahead.

That's how bomb techs got killed.

They headed northeast, speeding up South Broad,
toward the rough side of New Orleans and the Central Business District, Quinn taking the corners on
two wheels, the sidewalks still busy with a late-
lunchtime crowd of locals who flashed by the window in a blur. Ten minutes later, as the truck neared
the site, they were forced to a crawl on a street already packed with TV cameras and excited report-

ers, each hoping for some blood for the five o'clock news. Hannah cursed the milling crowd under her breath—half the thrill for the bomber was witnessing his chaos on television. She was convinced EXIT's number of calls would be drastically reduced if the nuts who made the bombs were deprived of their publicity.

With Quinn blasting the horn, they finally got past the media, and Hannah spotted the Metro Bomb Squad's rig, two blocks down. The two-ton truck carried the local team's equipment: their suits, X ray equipment, the PAN disrupter and demo kits among other things. It also pulled the TCV—the high-impact steel globe could suppress an entire explosion inside its inch-and-a-half-thick walls. All the techs had to do was pick up the bomb with their Andros robot, put the package inside the basket, then move the TCV to a safe place for controlled detonation. Contrary to the movies, no one grabbed the device at the last minute and tossed it out a window to save the day.

Unless, of course, they had to.

Mark cursed loudly and Hannah turned. He pointed to the neighborhood and she nodded slowly. It was a dismal and depressing place. A elementary school in need of paint sprawled directly across the litter-filled street from the TCV. The buildings were ringed by a chain-link fence, but in too many places to count, the wire had been pulled away and folded back to create gaps and holes. Gang graffiti decorated the walls.

On the other side of the ragged pavement, an even sadder building sat, fronted by a lopsided sign that announced Tiny Town for Tots. Built of concrete blocks with a low flat roof above, the day care gave off a shimmer of almost visible hopelessness. The windows were locked and barred, the empty playground filled with dilapidated toys. Hannah felt a wave of sympathy for the ''Tots'' who visited this ''Tiny Town.'' Their mothers must have felt the same way, but with no other options nearby what could they do? Another pang hit Hannah, this one even harder, but again she pushed it aside.

Spotting the commander of the local city team, she jumped from the SUV before Quinn had time to fully stop. Tony LaCroix had a little too much testosterone floating through him for Hannah's taste, but he did a good job. She decided he looked relieved when he saw the team this time, though. With EXIT there, he was no longer responsible for the situation; they were the feds. The other techs caught up with her as she reached Tony's side.

''Am I glad to see you guys,'' LaCroix confessed, confirming Hannah's suspicions. ''I think this might be the guy you've been tracking. I was just about to put in a request for assistance.''

"Give us the rundown," Quinn ordered.

NOPD-Central had caught the call about the suspicious box first, LaCroix explained, then a second telephone warning had come into the Metro bomb squad itself. The messages were the same, short and to the point. *There's a box by the back door of the Tiny Town Day Care. It's got a bomb in it. Tell them to leave from the front and do it now.*

The uniforms who had responded confirmed the caller's story. In the alleyway, leaning against the rear entry of the center, was a shoe-box-size container. Wrapped in stained brown paper, the unlabeled, lopsided package definitely looked suspicious.

"Everyone's out?"

LaCroix looked at Hannah as if she'd lost her mind. "Yes, Hannah. Everyone's been evacuated."

Quinn spoke. "Have you X-rayed yet?"

"There's not enough room to get the machine in there."

"So Arnold's too big, too."

LaCroix nodded at Quinn's assessment of the robot they used. "Way too big. Our mini's out of service and the four-by-four won't fit. The alley's less than three feet wide." A pained look crossed LaCroix's face. "We can't ray it and we can't bring the damn thing out."

"How about BIPing it?"

LaCroix shook his head at Mark's idea. "We blow that puppy in place, and the shit'll hit the fan." He jerked a thumb toward the back of the building. "There's low-income housing behind that fence. The mayor would have a cow."

Everyone's stress level increased. "Have they been evacuated, too?"

He nodded at Hannah's question.

"Then we'll have to try the PAN," Bobby said. "It's all we've got left."

Bobby was a specialist with the bomb disrupter. The device fired a variety of projectiles and was designed to disarm bombs without detonation. So far, they'd had no luck with it on any of Mr. Rogers's bombs.

"I don't think we can get it in there, either. The damn alley is so full of trash and crap—" Before LaCroix could continue, a minor riot seemed to break out near the perimeter of the cordoned-off area, then someone screamed—a piercing shriek that sent a sharp chill down Hannah's spine. She turned in time to see a black woman in a flowered house-dress push past a uniformed officer, her face contorted with agony.

Mark cursed again, and Hannah cut her eyes to Quinn. He was staring, too, but of all the people there, he would know what to do. He was great at his job, but he was even better with people. His ability to connect with them amazed her; Hannah would rather deal with a live bomb than an upset civvie.

The woman half ran, half stumbled to where they stood. Quinn stepped out to meet her and she collapsed in his arms, tears and sweat streaming down her face, her words coming so fast they were unintelligible. Hannah stood by helplessly, the same way, she imagined, Bobby felt as he looked on, his dark eyes rounded with concern for the clearly distraught woman.

"My babies!" the woman screamed, clutching Quinn's arm. She jerked a trembling hand toward the center. "My grandbabies are in there! They're in there! They're gonna be blowed up—"

Quinn's voice was low and calm. "We got everyone out, ma'am. The children have all been evacuat—"

"No-o-o-o," she cried. "They didn't get 'em. They forgot they were there. They didn't count 'em when they brought the rest of 'em out! Charles Junior and Sister. They forgot 'em both!"

Bobby sucked in an audible breath as Hannah felt her stomach constrict, a hot sickness suddenly turning her inside out. Above his beard, Mark's face actually paled.

Quinn held the woman's arm and spoke gently.

"Are you sure, ma'am? Are you *positive* they didn't just slip out—"

"Yes, I'm sure!" She flapped her hand behind her and the four of them looked over her shoulder. Another woman, this one younger and better dressed, stood by the uniform, obviously arguing with him. "Ask her! She's the one done left 'em there!"

Quinn called out and motioned to the cop to let the woman through. She ran to them, then spoke breathlessly, her eyes full of fright. "Two of the children are missing! We counted all of them twice, but Louetta—" she nodded toward the older woman in the flowered dress "—she came in late and I forgot to log them in." She shivered visibly in the cool January sun, her fingers knotting together. "They must have hidden when we left."

"How old are they?"

When Hannah asked the question, the woman glanced at her in a daze. "Charles Junior—he's five—and Sister." She gulped. "Sister's only two. She does everything he does. He—he probably told her they were playing a game or something and they hid. They've done it before."

"Where do they go?"

She turned back to Quinn, her eyes swimming with guilt and fear. "Th—there's a closet by the back...back door. They like to climb inside. It's where we keep the nap pads and blankets." She started to shake, then she gathered herself with a visible effort and reached out to clutch at Quinn's arm. "You've got to go in there, mister. You've got to go in there and save those babies."

LaCroix sent for one of his team members. She came quickly and led the two women away, making sounds of sympathy and doing her best to calm them. As they stumbled off, even more tension filled the space where they'd been, narrowing the choices the team had of how to proceed. Everything had changed. It was one thing when a building could suffer damage—it was a different situation when lives were at stake. Especially children's lives.

Bobby spoke first. "I'll go. This—"

Quinn interrupted. "No." His voice was firmer than usual and both of them knew why. "I'll do it."

"C'mon, man," Bobby persisted. "I know the area. I think I can get the PAN in there and then—"

"No. I'll go and get the kids, then I'll decide how to proceed."

Quinn felt the curious looks from Hannah and Baker as his authoritative words registered, but he couldn't take the time to explain. He hurried toward the SUV.

Hannah caught up with him as he swung open the back door. She grabbed his arm. "Let *me* go, Quinn!

Those kids won't leave that place with a man. I'd have a much better chance—''

"No way." He pushed aside his heavy protective suit. It took too long to get into. He'd throw on his SRS-5—a lighter outfit—and hope for the best. "They won't know the difference once I've got on the helmet."

"This is crazy, Quinn," she cried. "You can't just crash in there—"

"But you can?" His fingers found his jacket and he turned to her, holding it out so she could help him into it. She responded automatically, and he stiffened his arms as she put the coat on him, the protector hard against his spine, a trickle of sweat already rolling down his back.

She buckled him in and he saw that her hands were trembling. "We haven't done enough recon yet—"

"Hannah, for God's sake! We don't have the time for that." He plucked his helmet from the rear of the SUV, gave the plastic shield a swipe, then thrust it on his head. "We've got to get those kids first. Then we'll proceed."

"No," she said, almost in a whisper. "This is wrong…all wrong…."

He stared at her in puzzled surprise. Her face was flushed and her blue eyes were glowing with alarm.

She was the least superstitious, the most logical of them all.

Why this? Why now?

Lifting the visor, he reached out and tucked a strand of her hair behind her ear, the silk curl soft and fragrant. "Everything will be fine, baby. We've got a date tonight, remember? I wouldn't do anything to mess that up." He bent down and kissed her, the taste of her lips lingering against his own. Then he ran into the building.

He was barely over the threshold when the bomb detonated.

The blast was deafening, the force incredible. A shock wave of heat and light sent the back door flying, and then the walls. They exploded upward in a choking cloud of dust and debris, the roof immediately following with a shriek. Wood and metal, concrete and glass, toys and furniture—everything inside the building and outside for a twenty-foot radius was sucked up by the pressure. A moment later, a deadly shower of shrapnel rained down. The noise was unimaginable, then everything went quiet.

CHAPTER TWO

THE DOCTORS TOLD HER he might not live.

Describing Quinn's wounds in detail, they explained to Hannah how badly he'd been hurt. His right leg had been violently broken and a piece of metal had pierced his chest. The burns weren't too bad, but the blast injuries were severe. His hearing would probably return, then again, it might not—they weren't sure at this point.

For a week, she didn't leave the hospital. The nurses would occasionally try to get her to go home, but most of the time they left her alone, unwilling to face the battle she always put up and usually won. In the waiting room outside the ICU, she'd fall asleep sitting up on one of the chairs and have nightmares about the two children who'd died. The images haunted her and she suspected they always would.

Disregarding their own safety, she and Bobby and Mark had rushed in to pull out Quinn while Tony's team had searched the rubble for the children. Trying to stem the blood flowing from Quinn's chest, she'd looked up in time to catch a glimpse of LaCroix running out of the now-flaming building, a limp form cradled in his arms, another tech behind him carrying an identical burden. Bobby had followed her stare. When their eyes met a second later, his had been full of tears that spilled out and made two dark paths down his dust-covered cheeks. Hannah had wanted to scream at the heavens and curse, but instead she'd held her sobs inside and turned her attention back to Quinn. But every time she closed her eyes, she saw those babies again.

In the end, she left the hospital for them.

Hannah's mother had told her she should go to the double funeral, and because Barbara Crosby was usually right about things like this, Hannah went, stopping at home first to dress. It felt strange to walk inside her house and take a shower and put on a suit. She went through the motions like a zombie, eating the hot lunch her mother forced on her, then heading for the service.

The church was two streets over from the day-care center. Hannah drove by the devastation with her eyes averted, finally locating a parking spot down the next block. After turning the engine off, she sat quietly and tried to gather her composure, breathing deeply and counting backward from ten. It was a trick she'd taught herself years ago and it usually worked. But not this time. She hadn't even whispered "eight" when a couple walked by, obviously on their way to the service. The woman was already dabbing her eyes and the man had his arm around her protectively, his expression fierce with an angry grief.

If her mother hadn't been waiting at home, Hannah would have fled.

Instead she closed her eyes and finished counting. Entering the church a few minutes later, she took a seat and then lifted her gaze. The first thing she saw, at the front of the church, were the two tiny caskets. All at once, she wished even more desperately that she'd escaped when she'd had the chance.

Now it was too late.

Hemmed in by more than just the other mourners and a palpable grief, Hannah was trapped by her own emotions. There was nothing in life she wanted more than children of her own. Put in the place of the desperately grieving mother, Hannah thought she might have simply taken out her service revolver and ended her agony.

A wave of rising murmurs signified the entrance of the family. Hannah's initial view was blocked by others in the pew, but she could feel the heartache surging from the family members now moving down the aisle.

She got her first glimpse of them when they sat down. Like most of the mourners, they were dressed

totally in black. They filled two pews and part of a
third, the grandmother in the front row. Hannah
wanted to close her eyes against the sight. The poor
woman had aged ten years. Tears streaming down
her face, she slumped against the two young men,
grandsons, maybe, who sat on either side of her.
Beside those three, a mute, shell-shocked couple, the
children's parents, waited in silence for the service
to begin.

She'd learned the details of their lives from
Bobby. Beverly Williams, the mother, worked the
second shift as a printer's assistant at the *Times-
Picayune*. The father, Aloysius, ran a bakery, his
hours starting as hers ended. The grandmother, a
shampoo assistant at a local hairdresser, helped out
by taking the children to the day care before going
to work herself. They ate dinner together in the eve-
nings before the torturous schedule started over
again the next day.

Hannah could only wonder at the agony they must
be experiencing. The Williamses wore the stunned
expressions of people who'd been through an explosion themselves, their eyes blank, their faces empty.
Their world was gone.

The service began with a woman stepping up to
the dais behind the coffins. Quietly dignified and
impeccably groomed in a spotless suit, she introduced herself as the mistress of the ceremony and

welcomed everyone to the homecoming of the two children. After that, a young man seated at the piano began to play. A soft melody filled the church and Hannah instantly recognized ''Amazing Grace.'' But to her ears, the people around her seemed to be struggling to sing, their voices straining to maintain the song's hopeful message.

She couldn't even try. Instead she bent her head and stared at her shaking hands. One minute, those babies had been playing a game of hide-and-seek, and the next minute, they were gone. All the hopes, all the dreams, all the plans for the future that this family had for them…destroyed in one terrible moment. A moment designed by a madman.

She lifted her eyes to the caskets once more, where their shape shifted and grew. The white changed to mahogany, and instead of the Williams family sitting in the front pew, she saw herself.

Quinn's death or theirs? Who had decided? The minute she formed the question, Hannah knew the answer. There was no plan to any of this, no fairness, no justice. Those children died, but it could have just as easily been Quinn. Or her. Life offered no guarantees. All you could do was go out there, pray for help, then give it your best. Nothing else was under your control.

Hannah covered her eyes and fought her emotions. If she didn't begin to seek the things she held so dear—a family, children, a man to love—they weren't ever going to be hers. Things like that didn't simply arrive on your doorstep. They didn't come to you of their own accord. You made them happen.

Or you didn't. It was up to no one else.

Lost in thought, Hannah didn't realize the service was over until the pew began to empty. A few minutes later, she found herself outside, standing on the fringe of the grief-filled crowd now moving en masse toward a white-striped canopy. The cemetery shared the church grounds, she saw suddenly, and they were heading for the grave sites. She stopped, turned and walked against the flow. She couldn't handle any more. No one seemed to even notice; they continued toward the graves, moving around her like water surging past an island. She kept her composure until she reached the car, and then she broke down completely.

Back at the hospital, she longed to talk to the still figure beneath the covers, but she ended up saying nothing about the funeral. The following week, Quinn was moved into a private room. Staying beside him during the day, but sleeping in her own bed at night, Hannah walked a thin line of anxiety, torn between guilt and love. She knew she should leave Quinn—she needed to move on—but something she couldn't deny held her in place. Besides, he had no one else. She had her mother, but Quinn had already lost both his parents, and like Hannah, he'd been an only child. Hannah couldn't abandon him.

Quinn remained remote; drugged for the pain and deaf to all sounds.

She had no idea if he knew she was there.

HE KNEW SHE WAS THERE.

But little else registered. The days and nights merged together, and Quinn marked the passing of time by the level of his agony. His consciousness was a transitory thing, the pain a wave that pulled him into alertness, then sent him tumbling back out again. When he could think, he was sure he was going to die; when he couldn't, all he did was wish he would. He knew he had failed and the children had been killed. He slept as much to escape that fact as anything else.

After a while—minutes, hours, days—he wasn't sure, his awareness began to return. Slowly at first, then more quickly, images and sensations came to him. He smelled the smoke and saw a tiny shoe, he heard a woman's grief-filled scream and felt the heat. His body would eventually recover, but the grief he felt for the children was a wound that would never heal.

A MONTH AFTER THE BOMBING, Quinn was moved to a rehabilitation hospital.

Hannah continued to come every day. Always laden with messages from the other team members, she kept him abreast of their work and everything that continued to happen in the real world, including the fact that Bill Ford had left and appointed Bobby Justice as the new team leader. Quinn acknowledged the news with a nod and nothing more. Hannah had never learned of Quinn's promotion, but what did it matter now? He concentrated on her, instead. Beneath the mundane conversations, Quinn had begun to sense a growing withdrawal. Hannah was pulling away from him, and he suspected he knew why.

The team had suffered losses before this, but not since Hannah had joined. Ever since the funeral, she'd been quiet and subdued. She was grieving for the children, just as he was, and in true Hannah fashion had decided to keep her feelings to herself. He'd reached the point where he simply tried not to think about them at all. It wasn't a healthy way to deal with the situation, but it was the only way he could cope. The children stayed alive in his nightmares and that was more than enough for him.

But a week later, he decided the time had come for them both to confront the issue. Their emotions about the incident would only grow and eventually consume them if they didn't bring everything into the open.

He was reaching for the phone to call her when

his doctor entered. Six foot plus and built like a linebacker, Jorge Barroso was the best orthopedic surgeon New Orleans had ever seen. Born in Brazil, he looked as if he'd be more at home on a soccer field than in an operating room, but his hands were delicate and slight. They'd saved Quinn's life.

Dr. Barroso asked his usual questions, then made notes on Quinn's chart. After a few minutes he tossed the clipboard down and examined Quinn's battered body. When he finished, he pursed his lips. "I think it's almost time to kick you out of here, McNichol."

"Sounds great. I'm ready."

"No, you're not," the doctor said. "But we need the bed." He grinned at his own joke, then his demeanor went serious. "You still planning on going to St. Martin?"

Quinn's complete recovery would take months and they'd already discussed the fact that he needed somewhere quiet to recuperate. He'd decided that place was where he'd spent his childhood. An hour from New Orleans, St. Martin was a small town, up the river from where he still owned property that had been in his family forever. On temporary medical leave, he could retreat to the bayou and exercise until he dropped. Then Barroso would examine him again and reinstate him. Or at least that was the plan.

"Absolutely. In fact, I've already talked to the

physical therapist who lives there,'' Quinn said. ''He sounds pretty good.''

''He'll be able to help you quite a bit.'' The doctor's eyes met Quinn's, his brown gaze as direct as his words. ''But he's not going to make you into the man you were before this, Quinn. He's not a miracle worker.''

They'd discussed this before, too. Quinn tensed. ''I'm going to return to the team. I'm going to recover.''

''That's certainly a possibility. But you and I both know there's another one. You might *not* be able to work again. Don't pretend that chance doesn't exist, my friend.''

''That's not going to happen.'' Quinn's voice was level. ''I won't let it. If I work hard enough, I'll be—''

''You'll be fine,'' the doctor interrupted smoothly. ''But you might be fine while having a different career.'' He reached across the bed and tapped Quinn's leg. ''Your injuries were very severe. Your recovery, complete or otherwise, is not going to happen overnight. I don't want to see you in here again because you've hurt yourself trying to do something you can't.''

''*Can't* means *won't,* Doc.'' Quinn paused. ''I *will* return to my team.''

The doctor sighed then nodded, picking up the clipboard to make a final note. "I guess you can tell your lady friend you'll be all hers after next week." He shook his head and walked to the door. "*Qué mala suerte!* May God be with her..."

Quinn chuckled at the suave doctor's drama, but when the door closed and he thought about what was ahead, his laughter died. He *had* to come back to the team. His plans did not include staying at home and letting Hannah support him. Quinn didn't care what the doctor said—there was no other option.

His daily routine of meds and therapy began shortly after that, and he didn't return to his room until after lunch. Hannah's chair was still empty.

At six that evening she still hadn't arrived. He was trying to decide if he should call her when the door to his room opened. Assuming it was her, he smiled in anticipation.

Mark Baker and two more techs stepped inside instead.

"Hey, guys..." Quinn struggled to get up, but they all waved him down, each coming closer to shake his hand and say hello. Since his hearing had returned, the whole team had been in at one time or another, but surprisingly, Baker had been his most frequent visitor. They'd developed an uneasy friendship, partially, Quinn surmised, because he was now off the team, at least temporarily. His expertise and experience no longer posed a threat to the young tech.

Quinn watched the men situate themselves around the room, then he noticed they all looked tired and dirty. They'd obviously been on a call, but the usual, boisterous aftermath that followed a situation was missing.

"You guys been out?"

Mark sat down in the nearest chair and answered Quinn's question with a nod. "Yeah—some kids over on Toulouse got their school computers cranked up and learned how to build pipe bombs. They planted five of them in and around the mailboxes in their neighborhood and Metro called us. We went crazy trying to retrieve the damn things before somebody found one and blew off their freaking hand."

Quinn shook his head in commiseration as the other techs added their comments about what had happened. He listened, but all Quinn could really think about was Hannah. Where was she? Did her absence have anything to do with the men's subdued attitudes?

When the conversation lulled, he spoke casually. "Hannah go out on this?"

They took too long to answer. A warning bell sounded inside Quinn's head.

"She was there." Mark shot a look toward one

of the other men and a silent communication took place. Quinn had sent enough signals like that himself to know something was up.

"What happened?" he asked. "Is she hurt?"

"She's fine," Mark said quickly. "Just fine. But we had a little problem...."

"What kind of little problem?"

Mark glanced again at the others.

"Just tell me what happened, dammit." Still in his bed, Quinn managed to make the younger man jump.

"She dropped one of the pipe bombs," Mark blurted out. "But she's okay—she's okay, I swear."

Quinn's heart stopped for a single moment, then it restarted, the rhythm faster than it should have been.

"I take it she wasn't holding it at the time?"

Mark shook his head. "No, no... The Andros had it."

The men looked at each other uneasily. They were a team, and teams had rules, one of which stated you supported the other members, regardless. But this was different. Quinn had to know more, whether they wanted to tell him or not. He swung his legs to the edge of the bed, but as he stood, a quick knock on the door startled them all. It opened and Bobby was poised on the threshold, his expression grim, his demeanor unhappy. The men took one look and started edging past their boss, their muted goodbyes ignored by Quinn and Bobby both.

With the room empty except for them, Quinn stared at the other man, his mouth suddenly dry. Obviously there was more to the story than Mark had revealed. "What is it?" he asked without preamble.

"Sit down," Bobby said, pointing to the bed. "We gotta talk."

HANNAH SAT IN THE DESERTED bullpen, her head on her desk, her eyes closed. She was completely alone and the lights were off because everyone else had gone home to hug their kids and make love to their spouses.

She knew that's what they were doing because that's what she wanted to do. Almost getting blown up tended to bring out that need in a person.

She'd made a very stupid mistake tonight, and if things had ended even slightly differently, someone would now be knocking on her mother's door to tell her that her daughter was dead.

Hannah lifted her head and slowly banged it against the scarred and pitted wood. How could she have been so stupid? How could she have been so blind? In her time as a tech, she'd never come so close to making such a major blunder.

After the first bomb had detonated, she'd looked

at the pieces and assumed the devices were all identical. X-raying the homemade disaster, she'd seen the same thing she'd seen in the initial bomb, which confirmed—or so she'd thought—her assessment. She'd explained the setup to the other techs, then sent in the Andros to pick up the sawed-off aluminum baseball bat, lying next to the mailbox.

Unfortunately two different kids had made the bombs, and the second teenager had been smarter than the first. He hadn't inserted an ordinary fuse; he'd used negative pressure instead.

She'd misread the X ray. And then she'd mishandled the robot, her hand shaking from exhaustion. The machine had dropped the device. If the bomb had been a fused one, as she'd thought, it probably wouldn't have mattered. But it wasn't—the fuse was a decoy. The metal cylinder had landed on its edge and the plastic cap had flown off. The bomb had been aimed away from them, but by then it had hardly mattered.

It wasn't the kind of mistake someone with her level of expertise should make. It wasn't even the kind of mistake a rookie should make. One of the first things even a kid just out of bomb school knew was that each device had its own render-safe procedure. If he wanted to, Bobby could fire her and she wouldn't blame him, either. She couldn't believe it. What a mess…

She was too tired. Too worried. Too crazy. She'd been lucky as hell not to have injured herself or someone else on the team. She'd lost her focus.

She could have blamed tonight on the fact that she was grieving for the kids, but she would only be partially right. She *was* grieving—but not just for them. Tonight's emotions—and the sorrow she'd been feeling since the funeral—were also for herself and Quinn. Their relationship was over, and the day she'd fled the cemetery she'd known that. She'd only been staying with him because she couldn't leave. Not while he was still in the hospital. Distracted by that reality and full of sadness because of it, she'd nearly gotten in serious trouble tonight.

Dropping her head back down on the desk, Hannah closed her eyes and cursed.

"I DON'T WANT TO SIT DOWN," Quinn said. "I want to know what's wrong."

"Hannah screwed up tonight," Bobby said bluntly, falling into the chair beside the bed. "She hasn't got her mind on her job and she damn near blew us all to kingdom come."

Quinn sat down.

"Metro called us because the bombs were all inside or close to mailboxes. It seemed like a simple enough problem and we went straight out." Bobby shook his head. "Hannah was on her way here but she insisted on going with us first. The other guys have been trying to take up the slack, but with you gone, too, it's been hard.''

Quinn nodded. ''Go on.''

''I intend to, but let's get one thing straight before I do.'' He waited until Quinn nodded again. ''What I have to tell you never leaves this room. And I mean *any* of it. This is just between you and me, and if you ever tell anyone we had this discussion, I'll call you a liar.''

''Fine, fine,'' Quinn said impatiently. ''Just go on—''

''Give me your word.''

''You have it, okay? I swear I'll never tell anyone. Now, what in the hell happened?''

Bobby gave him the details the men had left out, his face etched with anger and worry. ''It shouldn't have gone down like that, Quinn.'' He shook his head. ''She botched it, man. Big time.''

Quinn defended her automatically. ''Working the robot isn't Hannah's usual thing, Bobby.''

''I know that, but Sid's out this week, too. His wife's in the hospital with kidney stones and he's stuck with his kids. Grandma's on the way, but in the meantime, we had five pipe bombs to deal with. I needed all the extra hands I could use, so when Hannah said she'd help, I said fine. But she aimed that Andros right at us, man.''

They sat in silence for a moment, then Quinn spoke, his emotions in a tangle. "This isn't good."

"No, it's not. It's not good at all."

Hobbling slowly, Quinn crossed the room to stare out the window at the parking lot. He was on the fourth floor, but the fog was so thick he couldn't see the cars.

"This isn't the first time she's screwed up, Quinn."

Something tightened inside Quinn's chest. He spoke without moving. "What do you mean?"

"She missed a detail last week in a report for Washington on one of those church bombings last summer. I caught it, but that's just not like Hannah. When I mentioned it to her, she got real defensive." He hesitated, then added, "She lost some evidence the other day, too."

Quinn turned around.

"It was just some minor stuff, but next time, who knows?" Bobby's dark eyes were filled with concern. "The truth is, I'm worried about her, Quinn.... I'm worried *for* her, too. Her mind's not on her job."

"It's on me."

"That's right." The other man came to Quinn's side. The light from the window glistened off his dark features. They stood together in silence and stared out at the fog.

After a while, Bobby spoke. "I was real upset when you got that promotion instead of me. I thought I was the better tech and I deserved it more. I even told myself there was some kind of racist crap going on." He shook his head. "But right now I'd dump the damn promotion any way I could. To the first man who'd take it."

Quinn spoke calmly, but he didn't feel it. "Why is that?"

"Because I gotta do something I don't want to do."

"And that is?"

"I'm thinking of firing her, Quinn. At the very least, suspending her."

Quinn tried to hide his shock, then gave up. He stared at Bobby in amazement. "Don't you think that's a little extreme? She made a mistake—we've all made them at some time or another. That doesn't mean she's not a good tech."

Bobby ignored his comments completely. "Are you going to quit or are you coming back?"

The question was abrupt and put Quinn on guard. He'd told no one, not even Hannah, that Barroso had warned him he might not be able to return. To tell someone, to voice the words, gave credence to the option and Quinn couldn't do that. "I plan on coming back," he said carefully. "Absolutely."

"Then both of you will be on the team again."

Quinn had no idea where Bobby was going with his questions. His uneasiness grew. "Yes, but—"

"There are no buts about it. Lives are on the line, here, Quinn, and Hannah's put them there."

"She made a mistake, for God's sake. A big one, yes, but she's only human. It's not like she dropped a pound of RDX in the middle of the bullpen—"

"And that damn well might be what happens next!" Taking a deep breath, Bobby started over, his voice softer. "Look, Quinn, the truth is she's never going to watch you go into another building without expecting it to blow." He held out his hands. "Put yourself in her place. Would you be able to let her go out again and not worry? Could you focus on *your* business and not hers?" His eyes narrowed and he shook his head. "It's only a matter of time, Quinn, before disaster strikes again."

Bobby didn't know it, of course, but Quinn had already put himself there. Hannah could have ended up in the hospital instead of him and that frightened Quinn terribly. The realization had made him even more determined not to leave orphans should that happen.

But he hid all that. She needed defending. "She's a professional," he said. "Once I get out of here, she'll be fine. Things will be just like they were before. We managed okay then."

Bobby kept his expression under control, but his

fingers gripped the windowsill so tightly his knuckles paled. "It's never going to be the same, Quinn. You've been injured severely and that changes things. As long as she loves you, she's going to worry, and as long as she's doing that, her life—and everyone else's—is in danger. If you don't care about that—"

"You're out of line," Quinn warned quietly. "You know I care—"

"Maybe, but I also know how these things work...." Bobby's eyes locked on Quinn's, regret filling their depths. "I value both of you, Quinn. You and Hannah are the backbone of this team, but I've got to take some action."

"Then suspend her if you have to, but don't fire her." Quinn clenched his jaw. "She worked hard to earn her position and she's damn good at it. The team needs her."

"They need the Hannah they had before you were injured. Not the one they have now. I was hoping you could help me fix this, but I see now that's not going to happen."

Bobby's attempt at manipulation ignited Quinn's anger. "If you expect me to do your dirty work, you can forget about it," Quinn said. "I'm not asking her to leave. She'd hate me forever. Besides that, she doesn't deserve to be fired. She's an excellent analyst and you know it. You'd never be able to replace her.''

''That may be true. But I'm in charge of the team now—the whole team—and I have to make decisions that are the best for everyone. C'mon, Quinn, can't you at least say something to her?''

Quinn shook his head. ''No way. It's not a good decision.''

Bobby started to speak again, then he broke off, clearly seeing the uselessness of his words. Quinn said nothing at all. Bobby stared a little bit longer, then left.

Quinn stood by the window, frozen with anger and confusion. A few minutes later, he watched Bobby exit the hospital downstairs and cross the parking lot to climb into his SUV.

Quinn's muttered curse filled the hospital room as he swung away from the window. Late that night, when everything was quiet again, another emotion replaced the defensive anger he'd felt for Hannah. Quinn lay in bed and felt fearful.

What if he was wrong?

What if Bobby was telling the truth? What if Hannah continued to work and someone got hurt or even killed?

The same guilt Quinn felt now—for failure, right or wrong—would then be hers, as well.

THE NEXT MORNING, QUINN made his way down the hall for his physical therapy, his mind on what had happened the night before. He'd still heard nothing from Hannah and that worried him as much as anything. An hour into the session, he was almost finished on the treadmill when suddenly his leg went out from beneath him. He was suspended for two seconds, then he crashed down—hard. The moving belt grabbed him and tossed him onto the floor. He gasped and swore as pain flooded his body. The last thought he had before fainting was that he'd dislodged the pin in his thigh.

Thirty minutes later, back in his bed, bruised and sore, he tried to rationalize the accident. He'd lost concentration and fallen down. Big deal. It didn't mean anything.

Did it?

Hannah arrived late that afternoon. He waited for her to say something about the call-out that had gone so wrong, but she kept her silence, her demeanor more subdued than ever. By the end of the evening, when she'd still said nothing, Quinn knew that could only mean one thing: she didn't want him to know what had happened. He couldn't press her and embarrass her more. When he urged her to go home and rest, she kissed him and left without argument.

Quinn watched the door swing shut behind her,

one question filling his head—what in the bloody hell was he supposed to do?

If he asked her to quit the team and she did, she'd resent him the rest of her life. If he'd ever had any doubts about that, they were gone. Seeing the guys and hearing about their call-outs over the past few weeks had taught Quinn that lesson. Hannah wouldn't be able to send him off to work every day and not go herself. She'd end up hating him.

He could say nothing and let Bobby fire her, but what kind of man would do that? Hannah had worked as hard as Quinn had to get where she was. If she ever learned he'd known about this and didn't warn her, she'd leave him.

Of course, if Quinn *couldn't* go back, none of this mattered one way or the other. He'd be forced to stay at home and watch *her* go to work every day. His only contribution would be his disability checks. Would they even be enough to support her and the children she wanted so badly? How would Hannah feel being tied to a man who couldn't do his job? Would her love turn to pity? He had no intention of seeing that happen, but what if…

It was a lose-lose situation. An answer didn't exist that wouldn't hurt one of them.

An ache went through Quinn's heart that made his physical pains feel like mere twinges. One of them had to give up the job.

The weekend came, and he still hadn't told Hannah he was scheduled to be released. As she prepared to leave Sunday, he pulled her to him and held her close. The smell of her skin was as heady as always. For a moment, all he could think about was how to prolong the inevitable. Then he accepted the fact that he had no choice, he had to say something. He looked down at her and tried to etch the moment into his mind, telling himself the words to convince her would come to him. He'd been able to find them a thousand times in the past—why wouldn't he find them now?

"I love you, Hannah."

He wondered about the sadness in her eyes, but dismissed it when she reached up and put her hands on his cheeks. "I love you, too, Quinn. And that's why we've got to talk...."

QUINN AGREED INSTANTLY and led her toward the edge of his bed, tugging her hand until she sat down beside him. Hannah's heart stung with a physical pain. In the past, she'd thought people were exaggerating when they talked about heartbreaks, but now she understood.

Lying in her bed the night before, listening to a hard rain pound the roof and thinking about the funeral, she'd decided the time had come. She had a dream, and if she wanted to fulfill it, then she had to set the plans in motion. *She* had to. No one else was going to do it for her. Not even Quinn, as much as he loved her and she loved him.

As she wondered how to explain this to him, he surprised her by speaking first. "I'm glad you want to talk because I want to, too. I've been thinking a lot about everything that happened. We have dangerous jobs, Hannah, and this has made me aware of that fact even more than I was before." He flicked his hand toward the hospital bed and all the medical equipment. "I ended up here...but it could have just as easily been you."

"I know that," she admitted. "In fact, I had my own realization...at the funeral. When I was sitting there, staring at those little coffins, I saw the truth. It could have been you lying up there at the front of the church instead of those poor kids." She took a deep breath. "I knew what I was getting into when I joined the team, but..." She shook her head. "I don't think I *really* understood until that moment."

He had twined their fingers together, and in the silence that followed he looked down at their hands. When he didn't answer or say anything, she reached over with her free hand and gently touched his cheek. "Quinn?"

He raised his eyes to hers, and something tightened inside her. She recognized the feeling as a warning, but for what, she had no idea.

"That's what I've been trying to tell you for the past two years, Hannah. Our careers aren't like anyone else's," he said. "And I'm not just talking about danger. What we do is incredibly intense. We have to be one hundred percent 'on' all the time. We can't accomplish what we need to with our brains half engaged—I've had friends who did that, and they paid for it with their lives."

"I understand that...now," she said quietly.

Since the accident, his voice had become harsher. The new tone made his next words sound all that more ominous.

"You say that, but do you really? I've been told your mind isn't on the job. You've been distracted by me and everything else."

She knew immediately where he was going and flared, not because he knew but because someone had taken it upon themselves to inform him. "You're talking about the pipe bombs, aren't you? Who told you?" When he didn't answer—and she knew he wouldn't—she went on, hiding her anger. "I made a mistake, Quinn, and I know it. I was waiting until you got stronger and then I was going to tell you about it myself. But I can promise you it won't happen again."

"You can make that kind of promise, sweetheart, but bad things can still happen."

She'd given the accident a lot of thought, and

when she'd calmed down, she'd come to see that was exactly what it had been—an accident. Everyone made them; she'd just have to be more careful. She looked at him levelly. "I was tired and I screwed up. I made a mistake, but that's all it was."

He stood suddenly. She did the same, and he reached out to grip her shoulders. Normally his touch would have brought heat with it, but this time a cold distance rose between them. Hannah shivered as another bad feeling rippled down her back.

"It was more than a mistake, Hannah. You could have been badly hurt...or even worse. If we're going to make this work, then something has got to change."

"Like what?"

He hesitated, then spoke carefully. "Maybe it's time for one of us to leave the team."

Her vague anxieties suddenly crystallized into something hard and cold. It lodged itself in her chest as she understood what had happened. Bobby was the one who'd told Quinn about the incident and Bobby was the one who'd put this thought in Quinn's head. That fact registered, then fled. Bobby wasn't the important one here. "Is that what *you* think should happen?"

"We've worked together for two years," he hedged. "I'd like to think we could continue. But..."

"But this makes you more sure than ever that we shouldn't have a family."

He didn't have to answer. The truth was in his eyes.

In the hall outside, a cart rumbled past. Dinner had arrived and was being distributed. Hannah felt nauseous as the smell of food wafted into the room.

Quinn stared and waited for her to say something.

"I can't do this any more," she said abruptly, rising and stepping away from him.

"That's fine," he said. "We can talk later if you like—"

She shook her head. "That's not what I mean." She waved her hands between them. "I'm talking about this. I'm talking about you and me. I can't do it any longer."

A stunned expression came over his face. "What are you saying?"

"It's over between us, Quinn. I want out."

He tried to reach for her, but she dodged his touch. He blinked, then spoke. "I understand you're upset. We've been through hell, but Hannah... C'mon. You're not thinking this through. We love each other. I need you and you need—"

She interrupted him, her voice like broken glass. "I know what I need, Quinn. And it's not the same thing you do. The real issue isn't about what we do or where we work, it's about who we are. And we're two very different people who want very different things. I knew that a long time ago, but I loved you so much I thought I could change you." She took a deep breath. "I was wrong."

"This isn't about our differences. This is about life and the realities that are out there. I'm not talking about having a family or children—"

"It's all connected, Quinn." She looked at him, pain filling her entire body. "I can't believe you don't understand that, as smart as you are about people."

"Hannah, you don't understand—"

"You're right," she agreed calmly. "I don't understand. And I probably never will. But I can't let that stop me from doing what I want to do. This life is the only one I've got. I want to live it." She swept her hand down his cheek, as her eyes filled with tears. A moment later, she was gone.

STUNNED BY HANNAH'S WORDS, Quinn felt the strength drain from his legs.

This was crazy.

Quinn loved Hannah. She loved him. How could she do this to them? How could she just walk away?

Even as he asked himself those questions, Quinn acknowledged he'd known all along this possibility existed. They'd argued too much for him to think otherwise. But dammit it to hell, children weren't a possibility for them. He'd lost too many comrades to think it couldn't happen to him, too. He wouldn't bring a child into the world just to abandon it. That kind of irresponsibility went against everything he believed in.

The door swung open again, and for one heart-stopping moment, Quinn looked up, thinking she might have returned. But it wasn't Hannah. One of the aides stood in the doorway, a dinner tray in her hand. She started to argue as he waved her off, then she looked at his face. Without saying a word, she backed quickly out of the room.

His heart felt as if it'd been winched from his chest and hoisted high. He'd never loved another woman as he loved Hannah. And with absolute certainty, he knew he'd never love anyone that way again.

But what choice did he have?

A clean break could set her free. Hannah didn't deal with shades of gray, so a black-and-white resolution—right or wrong—would give her the ability to move on. She could find a nice accountant, keep her career, have her children and never worry. She'd write Quinn off and everything would fall into place for her. She'd forget all about him.

He lied to himself and said it was for the best.

Her happiness was what mattered most. She could have her career and her family, too. Quinn closed his eyes, more pain—despite his resolution—flooding his heart. She'd share her life with someone who saw things as she did. Someone who could be there for her and her children. Forever.

Someone who wasn't Quinn.

CHAPTER THREE

Nine months later—October

"I DON'T HAVE TIME TO talk about this." Hannah stared across her bed at her mother. "I have to pack. I have to catch a plane to Florida, and once I'm there I have a bomb to examine. I *don't* have time for this."

Barbara Crosby's expression immediately closed, but not before a hint of hurt passed over it. "I'm only thinking of you, Hannah. And I'm only doing that because you never do. Ever since Quinn went back to St. Martin—"

"That's enough." Hannah threw a pair of black pants into her suitcase and slammed it shut. "Stop right there."

If Barbara had snapped off an equally angry reply, Hannah would have been pleased. Instead, her mother's eyes filled with something Hannah didn't want to see and she left the room. Hannah loved her mother deeply, but she had the feeling their experimental living arrangement might be more temporary than either of them had planned. It'd seemed like a good idea for Barbara to move in after Quinn had left town, but it also seemed as if they stepped on each other's toes a lot.

A strong urge to stick her head out the bedroom window and scream came over Hannah. Nothing in her life was going right. She let the reaction roll over her and then she pulled herself together, shutting out the self-pity. With Quinn gone, she'd come to the conclusion that emotions didn't pay. She had more important things to do with her time.

Like getting to Florida. Bobby had come into her office that afternoon and told her she was booked on a late flight to Destin. The name had barely registered in the aftermath of his explanation of why she was leaving.

Another day-care center had been bombed.

Hannah had kept her face a mask at Bobby's news. When Quinn had left her life, Mr. Rogers had moved in. And unlike Quinn, *he* was here to stay. Hannah had become obsessed with the serial bomber. She could put him out of her mind when she was working on other cases, but he was always waiting for her when she finished, teasing her, taunting her, just outside her reach. When the lights were out and she should have been sleeping, she dreamed of finding the sick bastard and dragging his ass to jail. Arresting the killer of those two children had become her goal in life. In a strange way, those babies had become her own. She suffered for them and she wanted revenge.

She'd find him or die trying.

Grabbing her suitcase, Hannah banged her way into the kitchen, the bag hitting every corner possible. At Hannah's noisy entrance, Barbara looked up from the stove where she was stirring a pot of bean soup that would have fed fifty. "Do you want something to eat before you go?"

"I don't have time."

Without comment, Barbara nodded and turned back to the range. Hannah waited awkwardly, unable to apologize but unable to leave. After a second, she sighed heavily, abandoned her suitcase and walked to where her mother stood. She put her arm around Barbara's shoulders, then spoke with contrition, some genuine, some forced. "Look, Ma...I'm sorry. I—I didn't mean to jump on you back there and I know you have my interests at heart, really I do. It's just that..."

Barbara stared at Hannah with eyes as blue as her own. She didn't remember her Norwegian grandmother, but Hannah was pretty sure the same bright gaze had come out of that face as well.

"That what?" Barbara asked. "That you want to never go out again? That you can't get over Quinn? That you still love him and always will?"

Hannah dropped her arm and stepped back, her voice as blunt as her words. "Quinn is out of the picture, Ma. I would have thought you'd be happy about that. Don't you want grandchildren?"

"Your disagreement about children isn't the issue and it never has been. It's just an excuse."

"I happen to disagree, but if you insist on believing that, then how about this? I don't love him anymore. That's not an excuse."

"You're right." Her mother paused significantly. "*That's* a lie. Otherwise, you'd go out. Lots of men have asked but you never accept. Mark Baker has invited you to dinner a thousand times—"

"And he can ask a thousand more and I'll still turn him down. He's not my type." She paused. "And I *don't* still love Quinn."

As if to reinforce the sentiment, Hannah made herself remember the night they'd broken up. Driving blindly, she'd made it to the end of parking lot of the hospital, then she'd fallen apart. Hot tears running down her cheeks, she'd pulled over and filled the car with deep, racking sobs, her misery too huge to contain. Everything she'd wanted, everything she'd dreamed of—all of it had evaporated in a flash. When she'd recovered enough to see, she'd made it home, but for months she'd felt empty and cold. Now that was her normal state of being. There would be no more tears. Not for Quinn.

Barbara returned her attention to the soup, staring into the simmering mixture. If she didn't agree with her daughter's pronouncement, she kept it to herself. Hannah leaned over and kissed her mother's cheek, then she picked up her suitcase and left.

QUINN ATTACKED THE FRESHLY turned dirt as if he was digging a hole to bury his thoughts. His physical therapist had recommended gardening as a Zen-like activity to aid Quinn's recovery and calm his mind.

The man didn't know Quinn very well.

Gripping the shovel with both hands, Quinn forced the edge deeper in to the sticky black dirt. Locals called it "gumbo," and it was an apt description. Wet, heavy and hard as hell to work, the soil rewarded those who persevered. When he'd first arrived, Quinn had gone to the feed store and grabbed a handful of seed packets and several flats of plants without even looking at the labels, then thrown the seeds into the ground with little attention and done the same to the plants. To his surprise, turnips had sprung up alongside pansies and radishes. Snap beans and green onions had taken root by the fence. In a few more days, he'd have fresh lettuce, too.

Eyes followed his movement up and down the weedless, perfect rows. There were renters now living in the home where he'd grown up. An older couple with grandchildren, they'd assumed he would ask them to leave, but that had been the last thing on Quinn's mind. He'd settled into the small overseer's cabin out back and asked only for solitude. Relieved but somewhat puzzled, they'd tried to visit with him in the beginning, but when he'd never cooperated, they'd finally understood he'd really meant what he'd said.

He wanted nothing but to be left alone.

Reaching the end of the last row, Quinn straightened his back and stretched painfully. From the bayou on his right, he heard the sounds of a quiet country evening. The lazy buzz of the cicadas, the distant caw of a crow, the soft slap of water against the dock. He was grateful he could hear them. Just as he was grateful he could almost run two miles, even though it left him gasping for air.

He had countered his isolation and pain with a storm of activity, spending the first months after the explosion either exercising to distraction or working the same way, pushing both his physical and mental limits. The EXIT team had conducted their own probe of the bombing, but they were busy and overburdened. Quinn had decided to help them out, even though they didn't know it.

And why not? he'd thought. What in the hell else did he have to do? His relentless pursuit of regaining his strength hadn't gone as smoothly or as quickly as he would have liked; in fact, it'd been a damn hard struggle with little to show for it. Investigating the bombing on his own had distracted him.

But over the months, he'd found absolutely nothing more than EXIT had, and in the past few weeks, he'd decided he wasn't *going* to find anything, either.

Since then, his only objective had been to stay awake. The minute he closed his eyes and went to sleep, the nightmares began. He had never seen the children after the bomb had detonated, but his imagination didn't care. Horrible images haunted him, anyway. The silent, open gaze of a toddler. The too-still arms of a little boy. A grandmother's wails.

He straightened and wiped the sweat from his forehead with a callused hand. Another memory haunted him, too. If he lived to be a thousand, he'd never forget the way Hannah had stared at him the day she'd left. She'd worn a blue blouse the color of her eyes, and the pain in her voice still echoed in his head. Along with the stupid little speech he'd told himself that night about their breakup being for the best. Who had he been kidding?

He blinked against the glare of the sun on the water and listened to the bees going to their hives out back, their buzzing recriminations loud in the quiet. At times, the memory of Hannah's last visit seemed more substantial than Quinn's actual existence.

In fact, sometimes he wondered if maybe he'd died and hadn't realized it. Maybe he *was* a ghost. Maybe he had departed this earth, left it as surely as the children had that day the bomb had gone off, only he didn't know it yet.

Leaning against the handle of his shovel, Quinn considered the idea once more, then he let it go and took up the tool again, slicing violently into the earth. He was crazy, not dead.

Only the living could feel this much misery.

THE FLIGHT SEEMED TO TAKE forever. Finally, the commuter jet Hannah had taken from New Orleans began its final approach to Destin. She looked out the window, but all she could see were twinkling city lights and then the vast darkness of the Gulf of Mexico beyond. A few scattered dots of light pinpointed offshore oil rigs.

The jet landed and Hannah collected her briefcase and purse, descending from the plane into a brisk night breeze. The air held the scent of salt, a fresh relief from the miasma that usually hung over the Quarter. The place looked nicer, too. Lining the walkway into the terminal there were pink oleanders and glistening palm trees instead of obnoxious drunks and passing hookers. What a change…

As soon as she retrieved her bag and entered the lobby, Hannah heard her name. She looked up to see Lena Canales waving at her from across the lobby. They didn't know each other, but Lena wore the dark uniform of a SWAT team and Bobby had told Hannah that Lena would be there to pick her up. Hannah acknowledged Lena's call with a nod and then started in the officer's direction.

Lena greeted her with open enthusiasm, taking one of Hannah's bags without asking. "So you're Hannah! I've heard so much about you EXIT guys—I was beginning to think you were a myth." She grinned upward, meeting Hannah's eyes. "But you really do exist, huh?"

The petite woman reminded Hannah of all the pretty girls she'd gone to school with who'd made fun of her height and boyish figure. But the officer obviously didn't act like them. Her greeting was friendly and made Hannah instantly like her.

"Whatever you've heard, it's probably not true. We don't save the world on a regular basis and our team members do not actually have supernatural powers."

"Well, that's too bad," Lena answered, her smile fading, "because that may be exactly what we need...."

They made their way through a crowd of retired folks and sunburned tourists, then went outside where they climbed inside a black Suburban, double-parked just outside the front doors. A dark, good-looking man sat behind the wheel, and Lena introduced him to Hannah as her husband, Andres.

"He's one of you," she teased, as they pulled away from the curb. "A fed. Thinks he's hot stuff..." The two of them exchanged a look that immediately filled Hannah with envy.

"I *am* hot stuff, all the feds are," he said in an accented voice. He shot Hannah a conspiratorial glance. "We have the secret handshake, no?"

His black eyes flashed and Hannah couldn't help but respond, jealous or not. "We *are* special," she agreed, "but sometimes I'm not so sure that's a good thing."

They chatted for a bit more, then Lena leaned over from the back seat where she sat. "Do you want to go straight to the site or would you rather start fresh in the morning? It might be kinda tough to see anything now."

"I'd like to go right now," Hannah answered, "but if you don't mind, I'd just as soon look it over by myself. I have a car reserved at the hotel. If you can give me directions, I'll go alone this evening, then meet you there first thing in the morning."

Lena nodded, then slipped a sheet of paper over the seat. "I went ahead and had a map prepared for you. I figured you'd need it one way or the other.

But I'll come in the morning and pick you up. I want to bring our team counselor and introduce you to her—she said she wanted to meet you. I think she'd like to pick your brain on how best to help the men deal with what happened.''

Five minutes later, Andres parked the SUV under the porte cochere of a modest motel. Jumping out, he came to Hannah's side of the car, opened the door and then took her overnighter. ''I can do that,'' she protested.

''Of course you can,'' he said with a gleaming smile, ''but permit me the pleasure of assisting you.''

Hannah relinquished the small bag, then followed Lena out of the car. The two women shared a look of amusement. ''He's Cuban,'' Lena explained. ''Just enjoy it...''

They laughed and went inside, where Hannah checked in. Lena and Andres left shortly after that, Hannah watching them from the sidewalk outside her room, the twinge of jealously she'd felt before growing inside her. Had she and Quinn ever had that kind of relationship?

The answer to her question was a hard one to accept.

AFTER SHE'D SLIPPED OUT of her black suit and into her jeans and a windbreaker, Hannah returned to the parking lot. Five minutes later she was in her rental car and following Lena's map. Initial impressions were too important to ignore, and with the distraction of others and their questions, she couldn't always concentrate as she needed to. She'd learned the lesson of how important focus was—Bobby had made sure of that by reprimanding her after the incident with the pipe bombing.

The map was excellent, and Hannah quickly found the small shopping center where the day-care center had been. Roped off with yellow crime-scene tape and lit up with portable lights, the area was easy to spot. A uniformed officer had been stationed to keep the curious at bay, but it was almost eleven and he didn't have too many customers. Hannah flashed her ID, then took in the devastation spread over the parking lot.

Or tried to. The debris strewn around was hard to handle. Tiny desks, scattered toys, books and games…everything she saw reminded her of the New Orleans explosion. Jumbled amid the wreckage was the usual construction material, as well. She mentally noted the position in the parking lot of various large pieces; it was as telling a detail as anything.

In the morning, the entire scene would be videotaped and logged. The results would go back to New Orleans with her, where everything would be noted, the distances meticulously plotted to a one-inch scale. But nothing gave her a feel for the bomb like seeing the site.

She didn't need the analysis to understand one thing, however: the power of this bomb was equal to the others. The debris field was roughly the same diameter as the one in New Orleans. In addition, the blast seat—where the bomb had exploded—seemed identical. Five hundred pounds of explosives had a lethal air range of roughly one hundred feet, enough to destroy a small sedan. The amount of explosive used here had to be close to what had been used before.

She sniffed the breeze, then bent down to look at a piece of charred wood. The burn pattern, lines of black and gray etched in the board, gave her as much information as the expanse of the field, if not more. She could be wrong—there was always that possibility—but she immediately ruled out any lesser incendiaries. It looked as if a high explosive had been used here, something like H-6 or Composition C. They were each mixtures of RDX, plasticizers and other explosives, and the eruption and heat they produced was unique. Very few people outside the military had access to this kind of powerful material.

Mr. Rogers always used it.

She stood, then began to circle the perimeter

again. Even though most bomb techs claimed they got "feelings" from sites, Quinn was the only person she'd ever known who really did have the ability to understand bombers. Hannah based her findings on what she saw—and what this bomb had left was exactly what she'd expected to find.

She stopped abruptly, her pulse taking a jump as she spotted something on the ground. Bending down, she stared with a puzzled frown at a burned piece of wire. The strands had been twisted one way, then they'd been brought back around and twisted the other direction. Twice. To anyone else, it would have been nothing more than a random bit of leftover filament, but not to Hannah. After putting on the latex gloves she had stuffed in her pocket, she gingerly picked up the wire, studied it then slid it into a plastic bag, carefully noting her time and location.

The Baggie went into Hannah's pocket and she continued her slow progress, careful not to touch or move anything else. She saw nothing more significant, however. She stopped twenty minutes later at the point where she'd begun.

Visible in the darkness, a smudged and badly singed teddy bear rested in the dirt a few feet away.

She clenched her hands. At first glance, this definitely looked like Mr. Rogers's work. The same kind of explosives, the same kind of target, the same kind of randomness...

But the wire troubled her, and so did the timing.

Until now, Mr. Rogers had kept to a schedule—one bombing every two years, always in January. Only nine months had passed since Quinn's bombing. Escalation was the mark of most serial criminals; eventually their needs grew and had to be fulfilled sooner and sooner, thus shortening the time between kills...or bombs. If this *was* Mr. Rogers, then he'd taken a pretty big leap.

But there was another layer here, she thought suddenly. Something she hadn't yet caught.

Every nerve on edge, Hannah looked around at the devastation, disturbed by the fact that she felt anything. Feelings had no place in her existence. But she couldn't deny this reaction. There was something evil here. Something dark. Something different from Quinn's explosion.

QUINN'S GARDENING HAD DONE nothing to calm him. A peculiar restlessness gripped him and he felt anxious and uncomfortable. By late that evening, he knew his dreams would be worse than usual unless he did something to head them off. At this hour only one place would be open, but he decided to go into town.

Actually St. Martin hardly qualified as a ''town,''

he thought as he crossed the bridge and entered the city limits. When he'd been a kid, growing up on the bayou, they'd had a 2A football team, a Dairy Queen and Stanley's Grocery Store. Since then, the school had consolidated with a nearby district, the Dairy Queen had closed and Stanley's had folded just like hundreds of other small grocers in rural areas, the shadow thrown by the superstores too big to overcome. The town had less than a thousand inhabitants now, and when the last of the Thibodeauxs and Boudreaus and all their elderly peers died, St. Martin would be empty.

Quinn parked his battered pickup down the street from Cherie's Diner. The joint tried to pass for a restaurant, but Quinn suspected they sold more beer than hamburgers, which was probably a good thing considering the way the latter tasted. Despite those facts, he went inside and ordered both, then took a seat in one of the booths, his back to the wall. Sipping the beer, he stared out the window and wondered about his anxiety, his gaze going to the metal newsstand on the sidewalk out front.

He stood up and fished change from his pocket, counting out the nickels and dimes as he headed outside. A few minutes later, he had the newspaper spread before him on the chipped table. He thumbed through it idly until he came to the state-by-state round-ups of news. For some reason, his eyes went straight to Florida. *Bomb Destroys Florida Day-Care Center. No Terrorism Suspected.*

Even though it was close to eighty degrees outside, Quinn felt himself go cold, his breath suddenly catching inside his chest. The print before him seemed to wiggle, the words growing too fuzzy to read. He sat quietly and willed his mind into stillness.

''Here's your burger, sugar. You wan' another Dixie to wash her down with?''

The voice of Cherie, the owner-cook-waitress, brought his attention back to the moment. She had put the plate in front of him, placing it directly on the newspaper, the oil from a dripping French fry darkening the print below.

''Yeah,'' he said, his voice sounding shaky. ''And bring me a shot to go with it.''

She sent him a curious look but took off without comment. He was pretty sure his wasn't the only boilermaker that had been ordered tonight, but he'd made it a rule to watch his drinking since everything that had happened. It would have been too easy to use it to ease the pain.

She came back before he could move the plate and start to read again. He wasn't sure why, but he waited until she'd passed through the swinging doors of the kitchen once more and then he read the article.

It didn't say much beyond the headline.

A bomb had gone off behind a day-care center in Destin, Florida. The locals were sure it wasn't terrorist-related but other than that, they weren't sure of anything else. They'd requested federal assistance in the investigation. No one had been injured. More details would be forthcoming.

Quinn didn't want to look, but his eyes went to the date at the top of the paper. The calculations only took a moment. It'd been nine months since he'd been hurt.

Nine months.

He pushed away the greasy hamburger and then the beer and whiskey, too, his stomach churning. He sat quietly and counted his breaths until they were even and slow once more, but when he looked at the paper again, the headline—and the date—hadn't changed.

He found himself rubbing his leg, the pin the doctors had threaded through what was left of his thigh bone suddenly hurting like a son of a bitch. He stopped and clenched his fist.

Closing the newspaper, he folded it and put it on the seat beside him, out of sight. He then pulled the plate of food toward him and ate every bite, leaving the drinks untouched. When Cherie came by and offered pie, he took a slice of apple, with vanilla ice cream on the side. He finished off with coffee, his mind as blank as he could make it.

Quinn finally stood up an hour after he'd arrived. He put a large-enough bill on the table to pay for his dinner and leave a generous tip, then he picked up the paper and tucked it under his arm. Nodding once to Cherie, he headed for his truck. It was the only vehicle still parked on Main.

He was halfway down the street when his denial took flight, something hot and sick replacing it like a well-aimed punch.

Pivoting into a dark and empty alleyway, he felt blindly for the brick wall, then leaned against it and bent over, throwing up violently, unable to stop. When he was too weak to walk and there was nothing left inside him, he slid down the brick and sat in the dirt, dropping his head to his knees.

He closed his eyes but it didn't help. The image refused to leave. Hannah shimmered in his vision, then she whispered her name into his ear.

CHAPTER FOUR

THE MORNING SUN WAS blinding as it shone through the curtains and into Hannah's motel room. Groaning at the light, she rolled over and focused on the clock beside the bed. Damn! She'd overslept and had only ten minutes to get ready.

The previous night had been a late one, but not through choice. She'd been up until after 3:00 a.m., unable to sleep, her thinking as twisted and confused as the wire she'd found last night.

She crawled out of bed and stumbled into the bathroom. In and out of the shower in minutes, she dressed rapidly and gave her last few moments to her makeup. With a what-the-hell-grimace into the mirror, she tossed her lipstick down and ran out the door.

Lena was waiting in the lobby, a dark-haired woman, neatly dressed in a business suit, standing beside her. They broke off their conversation as Hannah hurried toward them.

"I'm sorry I'm late," she said. "Too little sleep and not enough time…"

"Don't worry about it," Lena replied. "We just got here ourselves." She introduced the woman beside her as Dr. Maria Worley, the SWAT team's counselor. Hannah shook her hand, the woman's grip as steady as her eyes.

"Maria wanted to meet you," Lena explained as they headed for the doors. "She thinks talking to you might improve her mind-reading skills."

"Mind-reading…" The psychologist chuckled. "You bet, that's my speciality. One glance and I know exactly what someone's thinking…especially men."

They all laughed at her droll response, but Hannah's amusement fled quickly. "I wish you could," she said as the three of them climbed into the same SUV Lena had used to pick her up. "Although I'm not too sure I'd want to know what's inside this guy's head. I think it'd be pretty scary."

Lena put the vehicle in gear, her eyes catching Hannah's in the rearview mirror. "You went to the site last night?"

Hannah sighed. "Yeah, I went, but I almost wish I hadn't…."

Draping an elbow over the seat, Maria turned around to look at her. "What'd you think? We've never had anything like that around here before. It was devastating to the team."

"All explosions are devastating. Only the most

callous aren't affected.'' Hannah paused to look out
the window. The blue sky and perfect white sand of
the shoreline running beside the road seemed almost
unreal, especially in light of their discussion. ''And
it never gets any easier.''

A few minutes later they pulled into the parking
lot Hannah had surveyed the night before. The scene
looked even worse in the harsh sunlight. The three
women got out of the truck and stood quietly on the
perimeter.

The guard was gone. He'd been replaced by a
cadre of officers, each picking their way through the
debris. Hannah recognized their uniforms. They
were from the state bomb squad, and they were there
to help her catalog and film all the evidence. A stiff
breeze was coming in off the water and the yellow
crime-scene tape flapped noisily in its wake. That
was the only sound, however. The men worked silently, and the women said nothing.

Finally, Lena broke the quiet. She turned to Hannah and tilted her head toward the blackened parking lot. ''Any similarities to your guy?''

Hannah hedged, the length of twisted wire still in
her coat pocket. ''I'll be able to tell you more after
I get all the reports. It's not good to make up your
mind too early on in an investigation like this. First
impressions can be deceiving.''

Lena nodded with understanding, but Maria sent

Hannah a curious look. "You don't have a hunch about these sorts of things? Most law enforcement types claim they do."

"I don't believe in guesswork," Hannah said bluntly. "I look at the evidence. It's never lied to me yet."

The psychologist nodded thoughtfully, then Hannah headed off to begin her work. The woman's question seemed peculiar to Hannah, but shrinks were strange. At least all the ones she'd ever met.

The hours passed with a steady stream of officers coming and going, most of them SWAT team members who "happened by." They arrived alone or sometimes in pairs, each greeting Hannah politely. None of them left without talking to Maria. After a while, as Hannah watched, she began to understand the real reason Lena had brought the doctor.

The woman never made herself too obvious and she backed off quickly when the men became reluctant. At the same time, however, she was there—in every sense of the word—for each of them. Later on, Hannah figured, more than one or two would show up at her office to talk some more about the bombing. Just as Hannah had said earlier, the work was hard, even for bomb squads who saw the destruction regularly. There was something about the relentless power of explosives that etched its way deep into the psyche. Hannah had dealt with mental health people during other investigations, but she'd never seen anyone work a scene like Maria.

By the end of the afternoon, Hannah felt in need of the doctor's services herself. The more she saw and understood, the more crazy she became. Reminding herself of what she'd told Maria Worley about evidence, Hannah tried to temper her reaction and stay neutral. But it was hard. All she could do was wonder if the man who'd almost taken Quinn's life had struck again.

LENA ISSUED AN INVITATION to Hannah as they pulled up to the hotel after work that evening. "Andres got called back to Washington," she explained, "and Maria's significant other is at Quantico for training. We're on our own. We'd love it if you joined us for dinner."

Without thinking, Hannah started to turn Lena down, then she stopped herself. In New Orleans she had no close friends—she didn't have the time or the energy—but the notion of spending a few hours with these two women was suddenly very appealing. Maybe it was the stress of her discovery or maybe she just wanted to connect with someone instead of being alone with her thoughts tonight. Whatever the reason, she didn't care. "That'd be great. What time?"

They made arrangements to meet in an hour at a

nearby seafood house, then Hannah went upstairs with a weary tread. She wanted to turn off her mind and forget about what she'd learned, but she couldn't do that just yet. First she had to call Bobby.

It was late for him to be in the office, but he answered his phone on the first ring.

Hannah rubbed her gritty eyes and sat down on the bed. "It's me," she said. "I've been at the scene all day."

"And…?"

She spoke carefully, studiously avoiding Quinn's name. "There're too many comparisons to the other cases to ignore. My preliminary call would be to say if it's not Mr. Rogers, I'd be very surprised. I could be wrong, of course—"

"*Shit.* Since the timing was so off, I was really hoping for something else. Are you sure? The reports might come back with something different."

"They could, that's true. But he used RDX, or something damn close to it, just like before. The target was a day-care center, just like before. And he called and warned everyone, just like before. As far as the timing goes, all I can guess is that he's escalating." She paused. "Other than that, though, the signature's pretty clear."

"But we have to have proof."

"You'll have your proof," she responded. "One way or another."

Bobby started to say something else, then he stopped and waited for a police siren that was wailing in the background. In the pause, Hannah got a grip on herself. She was getting too wound up.

When the sound faded, she spoke again, her voice softer. "Look, Bobby, I don't want to jump the gun any more than you do, but the indications are fairly clear." She paused, then plunged in. "Besides the timing question, which can be explained, I only found one thing—so far—that doesn't fit."

"What is that?"

"I spotted a piece of wire last night. It was twisted on itself, twice. Mr. Rogers always *knots* his wires and he only does that once. Twisting is less sophisticated."

"It's one piece of wire, for God's sake, Hannah. It sure as hell doesn't negate the rest of the evidence, does it?"

"No. Not at all." Her voice was firm. "But there's something going on here that I don't like…."

Instantly regretting her words, she let her voice trail off. She'd mentioned Quinn's case only once since he'd left. Frustrated with the investigation, she'd brought up the possibility that someone who knew Quinn and hated him could have planted that bomb, not Mr. Rogers. She hadn't really believed in the impulsive hypothesis—no one had known he was going in there that day, of course—but she'd mentioned it to Bobby.

When she'd told him the idea was based on nothing more than a feeling, he'd straightened her out quickly. Quinn had been the one with "feelings" and he was gone. Hannah and the rest of the team should stick to the facts. He'd been right, of course, and that's what she'd done. Until now.

Bobby didn't even notice her slip-up, though. "I was hoping this son of a bitch had blown himself up somewhere." In a preoccupied voice, he went on, almost as if to himself. "Dammit to hell, this case has been a nightmare from the very beginning. And then it got worse. If those kids hadn't been in there... If Quinn hadn't gone in..."

"What was he supposed to do?" She couldn't help herself—Hannah flared before she thought about it. "Let those babies wander around inside a building with a bomb on its doorstep?"

Bobby came out of his trance. "That's old ground, Hannah, and we've covered it before. I shouldn't have brought it up—let's drop it."

"Of course," she said quickly. "That's all in the past. The only thing that matters now is catching this guy before he can kill somebody again."

"That's right. That's all that matters." Bobby paused, his voice now sounding weary. "Do what you have to, Hannah, then come back to New Orleans. We'll work it from here.''

THE THREE WOMEN MET at a place called AJ's, a small restaurant right on the waterfront. As they took their seats on an outdoor deck, Hannah listened to the lapping sound of waves against the dock and tried to relax. But she failed. Her conversation with Bobby had left her tense and uneasy, something about it nagging at her. She finally blamed the feeling on the fact that she'd snapped at him when he'd mentioned Quinn's name. She wanted to act completely disinterested where Quinn was concerned. Because she was, she told herself. He no longer mattered in her life. Catching the bomber who'd almost killed him had nothing to do with Quinn himself. It was all about the children.

"Have you guys got time to come by my house?" Maria asked as the waitress brought their check an hour later. "I've got to repaint the kitchen and I'm totally flummoxed by the color choices."

"Flummoxed?" Lena looked at Hannah and rolled her eyes. "You're the only person I know who would use that word."

"It's a good word!" Maria turned to Hannah and appealed to her. "Don't you think it's a good word?"

"I think it's an excellent word," Hannah agreed

readily. She'd deliberately gone out to dinner with Lena and Maria to get to know them better, and she'd spent the whole evening lost in her own problems. She had to snap out of it. "I'd love to see your home and help you pick out a kitchen color. No one should be flummoxed over something like that."

They laughed their way out to the parking lot, where Maria gave Hannah directions to her home. Within minutes, in three separate cars, they pulled up to a well-tended house in a quiet residential neighborhood. Hannah turned off the engine and sat for a second, staring down the street. She'd been envious of the closeness between Lena and Andres, and now another stab of the same emotion pierced her. Maria had a boyfriend and a home and a teenage son, too. Hannah struggled to get past the wave of longing that suddenly came over her. She'd sacrificed her relationship with Quinn to pursue having a family and she was no closer to that dream than she had been three years ago. Truth be told, she was further away than ever before.

It was a depressing thought.

Climbing from her car, she joined Maria and Lena, who were waiting for her near the curb. They started chatting as they went up the sidewalk, but before they could reach the front door, it flew open with the energy only a teenager could produce.

"Mom! I need to go to Randy's house! Right now! He has a new computer and I've got to help him or he's gonna crash and burn—"

"Hello to you, too, sweetheart." Maria leaned over and kissed the boy. "Can you say hi to the lieutenant and a new friend of ours from New Orleans—Hannah Crosby?"

He grinned at Lena, then shook Hannah's hand with a firm grip. "Nice to see you, Lieutenant, and nice to meet you, Ms. Crosby." Then he turned to his mom. "Can I go? I've done my homework and cleaned my room."

"Yes, you *may* go, but—"

Maria's agreement halfway given, he shot down the sidewalk and jumped on a bike blocking the middle of the driveway. "I know, I know..." he yelled over his shoulder as he pedaled away. "'Be home by ten!' I'll see ya then. Love ya, Mom—" He drew the last word out until he was gone from sight.

His overwhelming exuberance started them laughing again, and Hannah felt her spirits lift, in spite of her earlier gloomy thoughts. Following Maria and Lena into a comfortable den, she dropped her purse beside the couch. "I bet your son keeps you hopping," she said with a smile in Maria's direction.

"Yes, but in a good way. A few years back that

wasn't the case and we had some trouble. He's on the right path now, though."

She nodded toward the back of the house. "Let's go into the kitchen. You can give me your opinion and I'll pay you in brownies. I made them last night."

Over coffee and dessert, they looked at paint chips and made fun of the crazy names. After some good-natured arguments, they finally agreed on something called "Siberian Iris" for the kitchen walls.

Then the conversation turned to work.

"Do you do any profiling?" Maria topped off Hannah's coffee and then her own. "I've read a little about bombers but they're a real breed apart."

Nodding, Hannah picked up her spoon. "We don't depend on the method a lot, but since he's hit so many places, we have a decent workup on this guy."

"How many has he done?" Lena asked.

"Five that we know of—one each in Georgia, Mississippi, South Carolina, Louisiana…and now Florida."

"You're sure it's a man?" Maria lifted on eyebrow.

"Pretty sure," Hannah answered. "They usually are. There's a chance we could be wrong, of course, but we think he fits the typical profile of a serial bomber. White male, over thirty, under sixty, usually a little nerdy. For the most part, they're intelligent but underachievers, working in some kind of technical field. They don't like their bosses or their peers where they work because they're sure they're smarter than everyone else.''

"That describes ninety percent of the men I know," Lena mocked. "Especially the 'sure they're smarter than everyone else's part."

Hannah chuckled and Maria nodded her agreement.

"You may be right, but in this case, he usually *is* pretty sharp. But his girlfriend isn't. Bombers like women they can dominate, women they can beat up." Hannah paused. "A lot of times, they're wannabe cops."

"Which makes perfect sense." Maria supplied. "Officers are into control. I can see how the two would mesh. The psychological needs of a policeman melded with the dysfunctional goals of a lifetime abuser...."

"In English, please..."

"That *was* English." Maria frowned at Lena's comment.

"Not my kind. Try again."

Maria crossed her arms and leaned against the kitchen counter. "Everyone wants to feel in charge. We want power over what happens *to* us and *around* us. Dysfunctional people—those among us who have 'issues'—need an inordinate amount of control or their anxiety overtakes them. People in law enforcement are no exception.'' She paused and obviously organized her thoughts. ''They want to see—*need* to see—that life isn't random. They want to make sense out of the chaos that surrounds them.''

''But which comes first? Are cops like that or do people *like that* become cops?''

Maria's brown eyes darkened with approval as she glanced in Hannah's direction. ''That's a very good question, but I don't have the answer. All I can tell you is that's how they are.''. She smiled, then corrected herself. ''I mean that's how *you* are.''

Lena interjected something and the two women laughed. Smiling, Hannah nodded, but she had no idea what Lena had said. Her mind was stuck on Maria's last sentence.

''I mean that's how *you* are.''

The words reverberated inside Hannah's mind.

She *was* like that. She wanted to make sense of things even when logic wasn't present, and suddenly she prayed she wasn't doing that right now. Was she seeing signs of Mr. Rogers when they weren't really there? Was she being objective?

They headed outside a few minutes later. Waving

goodbye to Lena, Hannah started to climb into her car, then Maria stopped her.

She spoke softly. "Hannah, I just wanted to say if you ever want to talk about anything, I'd love for you to call me. Anytime."

"That's very kind of you." Hannah answered quickly, her expression as neutral as she could make it. Maria Worley made Hannah feel uneasy—her perceptiveness reminded her too much of Quinn. "I'll keep that in mind. Thank you for the offer."

"Of course, but remember one thing." The dark-haired woman smiled gently. "Whatever the trouble, it's never as bad as you think it is. That's an absolute proven fact."

They both laughed lightly, then Hannah drove off into the darkness. As she turned the corner at the end of the street, she hoped the good doctor knew what she was talking about....

CHAPTER FIVE

BY THURSDAY AFTERNOON Quinn had picked up his telephone three times. The first time he hadn't been able to dial the number. The second time he'd gotten the number half punched in and *then* he'd hung up. The third time, he'd grabbed the damn phone and thrown it across the room.

He sat in an ancient wicker chair on the other side of the cabin and stared at the hole in the wall where the antenna had gone through the plaster.

He was acting as if he were crazy. Or reckless. Or maybe just plain stupid. Probably all three.

He stood abruptly, crossed the room and picked up the phone from the floor, jabbing the number in too fast to think about it any more.

"Hello-o-o. This is Jolie. What can I do for you, darlin'?"

Long before he'd met Hannah, he and Jolie Bernard, a computer analyst for EXIT, had been lovers. She was a wild woman, a Cajun with sinful black eyes and long wavy hair. More times than he'd like to remember, he'd barely avoided her sometime live-in boyfriend. It was such a cliché he couldn't believe it'd really happened, but once Quinn had actually climbed out her bedroom window when the other man had come through the front door. He could still remember Jolie's wicked laughter as it'd followed him into the night. When her boyfriend had left her, she'd dumped Quinn. It hadn't been fun after that, she'd explained.

"Jolie…it's Quinn."

"Well, I been wonderin' where you be. My phone been quiet for almos' a week and I been wantin' to talk to you. I got news! Emile, he's moved back in! You wanna come back, too?"

Quinn couldn't help but chuckle. "You're too much for me, Jolie. My old heart couldn't stand up to it now."

"Oh, baby, we all done slowed down. I'd take it easy on you, I promise."

"I'll keep that in mind. In the meantime—"

"In the meantime," she interrupted. "You want to know what's up, right?"

They'd been talking once a week, more or less, since he'd left the team. Sometimes they simply chatted, but usually it was more than friendly visiting. Jolie had been Quinn's main source of information regarding the investigation. Making him wonder if there was more behind her teasing attempts to lure him back than she let on, she was risking her job but didn't seem to care.

"I want to know what EXIT's doing about the bombing in Florida. Is the team involved in that yet?"

He could hear her light a cigarette. She took a long drag, then answered. "I almost call you 'bout that, but I figure you'd call me when you ready... Yeah," she said. "Bobby, he done sent someone day 'fore yesterday."

"Who?"

"Who you think?"

Quinn's stomach rebelled against the three cups of coffee he'd had, a reminder of his reaction after he'd read Tuesday's paper. "Is she back yet?" he asked, his eyes closed.

"No." Another drag. "She comin' in tomorrow."

"Has she filed a report yet?"

"I'll check. If I find it, I bet you want it, yes?"

"Yes. As soon as you can, Jolie."

"Not a problem, cher. Soon as I find it, it's yours."

He hung up the phone and stared out the back door. He'd left it open, trying to catch a breeze, but all he'd attracted were mosquitoes. Their angry buzzing barely registered, however. All he could do was worry.

''THERE'S A NEW JAZZ BAND playing at the Shoreline tonight. What do you say we drive out there after work, listen for a while, then catch a platter of oysters to celebrate the weekend?''

Already cranky, Hannah looked up at Mark Baker. She'd come in late from Destin and she was in no mood for Mark. As soon as Quinn had left, he'd made his move on her and continued to do so even though she discouraged him. As she'd told her mother, Mark wasn't her type. He was too slick and too good-looking. He didn't seem real, and because of that, she sensed he had secrets.

''Not tonight,'' Hannah said. ''I've got plans.''

He sat down beside her desk, his aftershave wafting over to her. She resisted the urge to wrinkle her nose, then gave into it.

''I'm not *that* bad, Hannah. I *do* know how to show a girl a good time.''

She lied politely. ''It's not that, Mark. I don't have a problem with you—''

''Yes, you do,'' he said.

His candor surprised her until she realized he was just trying out another technique. She looked at him suspiciously.

''You have a problem with me and every other man who's asked you out since Quinn left. What's going on? Are you going to pine for that son of a—''

"I'm not pining for anyone." If she was wrong and his honesty was real, he was hitting a little too close to home. "I just don't feel like going out, that's all."

He studied her, his eyes breaching the protective wall she'd raised since Quinn had left. Then he appeared to give up, his usual grin replacing the apparent sincerity. "You need a good man, Hannah. I could help you out—"

Relieved by his regression, she answered him without delay. "What *you* need to concentrate on is your work, not me." She nodded toward the papers on her desk. "I'm still waiting for that file on the bombing in Georgia, not to mention the one in Mississippi. Your time would be better spent locating those like I asked you to instead of trying to get me to go out with you."

He stood, unfazed by her blunt dismissal. "You wouldn't say that if you'd just relax and let me show you a good time. You might be surprised by how much you'd enjoy it."

She didn't look up from her desk. "Go away, Mark," she said. "Leave me alone and do your work."

A few minutes later, she sensed a presence again. Studying her file, she said, "I haven't changed my mind. Go away."

"That's no way to talk to your mother."

Hannah jerked her head up. Barbara was standing in front of her desk. "God, Ma, I'm sorry...." Hannah rocked back in her chair. "I didn't know it was you. Mark was here a second ago, bugging me, and I thought he'd come back."

Barbara stepped up to Hannah's desk, opened the plastic sack she held and pulled out a small ivy, replacing the dead one on the corner of the desk, which she'd brought Hannah the month before. The plants never lived because Hannah didn't water them. She didn't have the time or the interest, but in a way, it didn't matter. Her brown thumb gave Barbara something to do.

She finished fussing with the ivy, then looked at her daughter with an irritated expression. "So you turned him down again."

"Yes, Ma. I turned him down again."

"You're gonna die a lonely old woman."

"I certainly hope you're wrong about that, but if you're not, then that's how it'll be." Hannah smiled with a fake brightness. "Thank you for the new plant. You want to sit down and visit for a while?"

"No."

"Well, what's your hurry?" Hannah asked. "I thought I might take you out to lunch." Actually the idea had just occurred to her, but it sounded like a good one.

"I can't go to lunch with you. I have other plans."

"Other plans?"

"Lindsey suggested we go to the Acme for lunch. After that we might drop in at the casino."

Although they'd drifted apart after high school, Lindsey Bismarc and her mother had been fast friends forever. Following the death of Hannah's stepfather a few years back, the two women had become quite close again. They saw each other at least once a week. The casino was a new addition to their slate of activities and Hannah was thrilled. Like the plants, it served to divert Barbara's attention from Hannah's love life...or lack thereof.

Barbara left a few minutes later.

Hannah went back to her work, but not for long. Bobby appeared ten minutes after her mother had gone, clutching a sheaf of files, his tall frame filling the space between Hannah and the rest of the bullpen. They'd spoken, but only briefly since she'd returned, their time taken up by other tasks.

"The reports just came in from Florida," he said. "Have you seen them yet?"

"No," she said. "I haven't even logged on today I've been so busy."

"Then I'll give you the executive summary. You were one-hundred-percent correct. Initial reports confirm the explosive mixture used in Florida is identical to the stuff that was used here and every-where else.''

''And the wire I found?''

He flipped through the report, read something, then looked up at her. ''Inconclusive. The debris report says some explosive residue was present but only in trace amounts. Impossible to say for certain the wire was even part of the bomb.''

She would have liked a more definitive resolution, but Hannah had learned she seldom received the black-and-white answers she wanted. She had to give more weight to the unequivocal points, like the explosives, and accept that the wire had to have been an anomaly that meant nothing.

Bobby took the chair by her desk and they went over the report in detail. An hour later, there was no way to dispute any of the findings.

Hannah swung around and looked out the nearest window. Her desk was in the corner of the bullpen and on a clear day she could make out the steeple of the cathedral. But not today. The sky was dark and hollow-looking, a visible reflection of how she felt inside.

''God, I wish…'' She didn't realize she had spo-ken out loud until it was too late.

Bobby eyed her curiously. ''Wish what?''

''Nothing. It doesn't matter.''

For a second, it appeared as if he wanted to press

her, but then he stood, thank goodness. How could she have explained to him what she'd almost said? That for a minute she'd wished Quinn was here to help. His insights had always been so great....

Bobby stopped in the doorway and looked back at her. "Was that your mother I saw in here a minute ago?"

"I'm afraid so."

"She still bugging you to get a social life?"

"Of course. It's the only record she can play."

He'd been as bad as her mother since Quinn had left and she knew what was coming next. "You don't listen too good, do you? All them bomb explosions ruin your hearing? I thought you and I had talked about you getting on with your life. Janie's still waiting. One of those hotshot lawyers she works with needs a lady to grace his arm."

Bobby's wife, a fledgling attorney at a local law firm, had been trying to fix up Hannah for months. Hannah had gone out several times with different possibilities, but in the end she'd stopped, explaining to the woman that she moved in circles too rich for Hannah's blood. Overly impressed with her associates and their wives, Janie tried hard to wear the right clothes and go to the right places. She'd even insisted their daughter, Denise, attend the local Catholic school, an extravagance that had to cost Bobby a small fortune each month.

"Janie's swearing she's got the perfect one picked out."

"The perfect one?" Hannah shook her head. "Tell her I appreciate the effort, but I don't believe in perfect anymore."

JOLIE CAME THROUGH as she always did. A week later, Quinn got Hannah's full report, including copies of her handwritten notes. The precise, even lettering stopped him for a moment. All he had to do was close his eyes and he could see her chewing the end of the pencil and frowning, her concentration total and complete. She never did anything halfway.

Including making love to him.

He'd battled his memories endlessly since he'd left New Orleans. Sometimes he won, but mostly he lost. When he did, along with a thousand other painful memories, he could have sworn he felt the imprint of Hannah's hands on his body, the touch of her lips against his own. He felt as if he were missing something necessary for him to live—like air.

He shook his head to dislodge the thought and the images. An hour later, he pushed the scattered papers into a messy pile and rose from the desk he'd put in his spare room, the sick feeling he'd had in his gut since reading the newspaper coming back full force.

Something was wrong.

Something—he didn't know what—was very, very wrong.

Quinn could smell it, hell, he could almost taste it. Day by day, as he'd thought more about it, he'd come closer to what that something was. The total picture was still out of focus—a snapshot with blurred edges—but a whole he hadn't seen before was beginning to emerge.

The physical signatures of the bombings were identical, and Hannah had made the logical conclusion anyone studying the evidence would have. But the timing was off between New Orleans and Florida. And even more disconcerting, people had died in New Orleans but not Florida.

Did Hannah see the significance of those two facts? They were extremely important to the psychology of Mr. Rogers. With her penchant for the literal, he'd bet money she'd caught the discrepancy but hadn't completely understood its importance. She was one very smart lady…but not in that particular way. He almost wished he didn't get it, either; the possibility it brought to mind stunned him.

He debated with himself until after lunch, then he couldn't wait any longer. He picked up the phone and dialed. It rang for so long he was just about to hang up when Barbara's breathless ''hello'' came over the line. For an instant he was confused, then he figured it out. Concentrating on what he was going to say instead of what he was doing, he'd dialed the house, not Hannah's office.

"Hello?" Barbara repeated.

"Barbara—it's Quinn McNichol."

"Oh, Quinn…I just came through the door. I've been out with Lindsey."

Quinn had always liked Hannah's mother, and he'd been happy to learn from Jolie that she'd moved in with Hannah. She would look after her daughter and tend to those things that Hannah forgot about, like eating.

"It's good to hear from you," she said. "When are we going to see you again?"

He smiled at her bluntness. Hannah hadn't come by her plain-speaking on her own.

"Sooner than Hannah might like," he replied. "That's why I'm calling, but I should have dialed the office. Since I've got you, though, I was wondering—"

"How she is?" Interrupting him, Barbara supplied the question and answer all in one breath. "She's working herself to death, that's how she is. She doesn't come home before eight or nine and she's always on an airplane going somewhere. She never relaxes, Quinn. Never. She works constantly so she won't have to think."

"About what?"

"You, what else?"

Quinn fell silent, his heart thudding before he realized what was going on. He spoke gently. "Is that her explanation, Barbara, or your interpretation?"

"My own, of course. But I know my daughter, Quinn, and I know how she feels about you."

Quinn didn't doubt what Barbara believed. But this time she was wrong. Hannah had made that very clear. "Is she there?" he asked pointlessly.

"No. She's at work. Just like I said." She switched gears abruptly. "Are you well?"

"I'm getting there." The lie hurt—almost as much as his leg, which didn't seem to be getting a whole helluva lot better. He wasn't about to admit that to anyone, however.

"Then when are you coming back?"

"I'm not sure yet," he hedged. "It shouldn't be much longer."

Barbara shared another quality with Hannah, he remembered a moment later. She suffered no fools. "Well, maybe you better see if you can hurry up," she said sharply. "My daughter needs you, Quinn, whether she knows it or not."

SHE HAD A MOUTHFUL OF a three-day-old Krispy Kreme doughnut—her dinner—when the phone on her desk rang. Swallowing fast, Hannah picked up the receiver and mumbled something close to hello.

The voice at the other end shocked her so much she almost choked.

"Hannah?"

"Quinn," she finally managed to say.

"Can you talk or are you busy?"

She looked at her desk. On one side, papers were strewn haphazardly, spilling from folders and envelopes. On the other side, bits and pieces of twisted wire and burned metal mingled with scraps of singed material and plastic bags full of more evidence. It was almost nine o'clock and she had three more reports to write before tomorrow morning.

"I was just about to leave," she said. "I have a date tonight. For dinner. And a late concert," she added. "At a jazz club."

He didn't hesitate, and she felt a twinge of disappointment that she immediately labeled indigestion. She pushed the rest of the doughnut into the trash can.

"I won't keep you long, then," he said, his deep voice rippling over her. "I just wanted to ask you about the case in Florida. I read about it in the paper."

She shouldn't discuss the case with him. Technically he was a civilian and she'd be breaking confidentiality. But this was Quinn. She answered before she could give it more thought.

"I believe it's him," she said brusquely.

His voice stayed level and calm. "Are you sure?"

"No. Nothing is ever sure in this business. But the explosives match. And the trigger setup looks identical." She paused. "I'll put it like this—we've seen nothing that contradicts his signature."

The silence on Quinn's end of the phone was so complete, she could hear a nightbird crying somewhere out on the water. The echoing sound reminded her of a Sunday afternoon a few years back when they'd visited his family home. She'd imagined their children playing on the edge of the bayou.

"What about the timing? Have you checked—"

His voice shattered the memory. She spoke sharply, gripping the phone with both hands. "I *know* the timing's off and I also know how to do my job. I'd appreciate it if you didn't call me up and question that."

"That's not what I'm doing—"

"Then what *are* you doing? Why did you call?"

"I need to see you, Hannah."

She counted to five, then spoke. "Why?"

"I'd rather not explain right now," he hedged. "Can you come out here this weekend?"

"Why don't you come here?"

"Because this is a conversation that should be held in private."

"Well, I'm not driving out there unless you tell me why first."

"Don't make this harder than it has to be."

His voice had gone husky, and sitting behind her lonely desk in a building that was way too quiet, she imagined his coal-black eyes and disheveled hair. He never had time to get it cut, but somehow the careless look went well with the shadow of a beard he always had. Did he have on his jeans? And an open white shirt with the sleeves rolled up? All the lonely nights had left her aching for Quinn's touch, and suddenly her body remembered what her heart wanted to forget.

All of which she put aside with hard resolution. "I don't believe I understand," she said stiffly.

"And I don't believe you're being such a tight-ass." His voice filled with irritation. "This is important, Hannah. I need to see you, and I don't want to come there—we need some privacy for this conversation. Why in the hell can't you just bend a little and do what I'm asking?"

Her throat seemed to close at his words, the back of it beginning to sting. Maybe she was getting something. "Why in the hell can't you just tell me what you want?"

He took so long to answer, she heard the nightbird again. Finally he replied. "It's about the case, Hannah. I have to talk to you about Florida. I think there's a possibility of something going on down there that none of us have considered. I hope like hell I'm wrong, but if I'm not…you've got a major problem on your hands."

CHAPTER SIX

SHE DIDN'T KNOW HOW it came about, but by the time she hung up, Hannah had agreed to drive out to St. Martin on Saturday morning. Navigating the New Orleans traffic home that night, she vented her frustration with a muffled scream, then banged her fist against the wheel, earning a suspicious glance from the driver one lane over, who promptly locked her car door.

Why had Hannah promised to do that? Was she crazy? Had the past few months been so stressful she'd finally begun to crack?

Seeing Quinn would be a huge mistake, but she hadn't been able to say no when he'd said what he did. Refusing to tell her specifics, he'd sounded ominously certain that he knew something she didn't.

But was that the real reason she'd agreed to see him? Sure, she was obsessed with Mr. Rogers, and sure, she wanted to clear the case, and sure, there were plenty of excellent reasons to check this out. Hell, she'd even wished for his help the other day while talking to Bobby. But now she wasn't so sure.

Maria's words came back to haunt her. *"People in law enforcement are no exception. They want to see—need to see—that life isn't random. They want to make sense out of the chaos that surrounds them."*

Was that what Hannah was doing? Was she trying to put logic into the equation between her and Quinn?

She did her best to set aside her doubts, but the week passed in slow motion, a torturous interlude that she filled with work to keep Quinn out of her thoughts. The closer Saturday came, the more irritable Hannah grew. After snapping at Bobby on Friday when he asked if she'd like some coffee, Hannah knew she had to get out of the office.

She drove home, put on something comfortable and went straight into the kitchen. The house felt lonely and quiet on Fridays, which was Barbara and Lindsey's bingo night, but for a change, Hannah was glad she was by herself. She'd ducked her mother's questions all week long—if she'd had to continue the charade tonight she might have exploded.

Going to the utility room, Hannah pulled out the mop, the vacuum cleaner and a basket full of cleaning supplies and went to work.

After three hours, she felt some relief, satisfaction coming over her as she stared at the sparkling kitchen and shiny floor. She put away the vacuum and supplies, then stepped outside. The night air was humid, the fog so thick it misted her skin and left tearlike droplets clinging to her eyelashes.

She brushed them away and told herself tomorrow was just like any other day. She'd see Quinn, listen to whatever he had to say, then she'd come back to New Orleans and forget about him. Again. They wanted different things out of life and they always would.

With that fact firmly in mind, Hannah returned to the kitchen. Rummaging in the refrigerator, she pushed past the salad and casserole her mother had left for her and found a block of cheese and some strawberry yogurt. She ate the yogurt out of the container while she sliced off a chunk of the cheese. Grabbing some crackers from the cabinet, she finished her gourmet meal standing by the now-polished kitchen counter. She went to bed, but she didn't go to sleep.

QUINN WASN'T A VAIN MAN; he didn't make it a habit to study himself in the mirror. But Saturday afternoon, as he stared at his reflection, all he could do was shake his head. He had yet to regain the weight he'd lost after the accident, and he was beginning to think he never would. His arms and legs, once beefy and strong, were now hard and lean, his cheeks two blades where before they'd been full. He couldn't decide if he looked better or worse, but he knew one thing for certain.

He definitely looked older.

A big reason for that was his hair. It had begun to gray, a large streak of it particularly noticeable at his left temple. The change didn't bother him, but he had been surprised by the stubble on his cheeks. It was almost completely white. He ran his hand over his jaw, feeling the roughness. He hadn't planned on shaving, but suddenly he decided he would and hastily grabbed his razor. He was shaking off the last bit of soap when the crunch of a car's wheels sounded on the drive outside.

His heart thumped as he walked out of the bathroom and straight to the front porch, his shirttail hanging out. He stepped off the porch and into the sunshine, slinging the soapy towel he'd inadvertently brought with him over his shoulder.

Hannah shut off the car but made no move to get out. Through the windshield, he could see her sitting quietly. She was counting down and getting herself together. He'd seen her do it a thousand times…but never when all she had to face was him. The realization made him pause, a fresh wave of sadness hitting him.

After a full minute had passed, she opened the car door and climbed out. The sun was behind her and he couldn't see her face. However, he could read her body so well, he didn't need to see her expression to know what she was feeling. When she got close, she stopped abruptly, and in the still morning air, he caught her murmur of surprise before she could cut it off. She was shocked by his appearance.

She didn't try to hide her reaction as he came closer. And for that, he loved her even more.

"You weren't expecting an old man," he said bluntly.

Anyone else would have protested and tried to cover up, but not Hannah. It wasn't her style, and she couldn't have carried off the deception if she'd wanted to. Her blue eyes studied him unmercifully, her gaze burning its way across his features and gray hair. "You do look…different."

He wanted to bullshit her, but Hannah wasn't the kind of woman he could do that to. She'd call him on it, straight and fast. "It's been tough," he admitted. "The physical therapy…is taking longer than I expected."

She regarded him with a serious expression. "Is that why you called me?"

"No. Let's go inside and I'll explain." He tilted his head toward the road beside his cabin and the big house at the end of it. "We'll give the old folks something to talk about."

She came toward him and he turned, both of them starting for the porch at the same time. When she reached the top and he was still on the second step she looked back, her eyes more troubled than before. "Do you...need some help?"

He ran every day, but the stairs still presented a challenge. He shook his head and patted his leg. "It'll get me there—I just need a bit more time than I used to."

She nodded, then waited for him, looking as if she wanted to do something for him but didn't quite know what. He finally got to the top and then they went inside together.

HANNAH SAT IN AN ANCIENT wicker chair and waited for Quinn. He'd insisted on getting her something to drink, and he'd gone into the kitchen to get it. She stared out at the bayou and tried to stop her trembling.

The last time she'd seen him—even with the bandages and the cast—he'd looked wounded, but he'd still been himself. When she'd pulled into the drive and seen him waiting for her, for a minute she'd actually wondered if she had gotten lost and turned into a stranger's house. He'd changed so much he was almost unrecognizable. He seemed to have been pared down to his essence, his face and body lean and hard. Even the streak of gray in his hair added to the impression. It was like marble, and it made him look that way, too. Cold and imposing.

Then she'd stared some more.

And she saw the truth. Underneath the surface, he hadn't changed a bit. His eyes were as dark and probing as they'd always been, his lips as full and sensual. The air of quiet confidence and power that had always surrounded him was as strong as ever.

He was still Quinn.

Beyond even these immediate attributes, however, something else told her he was the man she'd always known. She hated to acknowledge what that something else was, but it couldn't be ignored.

Looking at him as he'd stood in the sunshine, his shirt untucked, that towel over his shoulder, his jeans unbuttoned...oh, God. That vein of gray in his hair, those lines down his now-craggy face, the lean and narrow hips—in reality, the changes had only added to his attraction.

Her desire for him had reached out and pulled her closer and closer. No one but Quinn could affect her that way. No one but Quinn could satisfy that need, either.

Pushing her thoughts aside, Hannah looked around for something else to focus on. Her eyes landed on the wall beside the front door where he'd hung his blue-ribbon certification credential. Techs across the world attended the school that was run by the Explosives Unit—Bomb Data Center wing of the FBI. It was a five-week course and they had to go every three years. The last time Quinn had gone, she'd met him afterward and they'd slipped off to Bermuda. A thought that brought her right back to where she'd been before. They'd only left the room to eat, and sometimes they'd forgotten to do that.

Quinn returned, but his appearance only served to turn up the heat growing inside her. She reached for the iced tea he handed her and drank the glass in one gulp.

"Would you like some more?" he asked politely.

A variety of answers came to her mind, but none of them had anything to do with iced tea. "No, thank you," she said, and left it at that.

He took the chair next to hers and wasted no time. "I want to hear about the case in Florida."

"Why?"

"I'll explain in a minute, I promise. You go first."

Still stunned by her response to him, Hannah acquiesced. "All right...I'll tell you, but you have to keep that promise. Technically, I shouldn't be letting any of this information out. You know that as well as I do."

He waved aside her words.

She clutched the empty glass and began to talk. Without conscious effort, she fell into the rhythm of an EXIT report, outlining the facts and supplying the evidence points as if they were having a review. A full hour passed before she finished.

He had stood up at some point in her narration and moved to the window. He turned now as she finished speaking. His voice, full of tension, drew her in. "When was the bombing in Georgia?"

"Six years ago, January."

"And Mississippi?"

"Four years ago, January."

"South Carolina?"

"Two years ago, January."

"Notice a pattern?"

She frowned with obvious annoyance. "Of course there's a pattern, Quinn. We talked about that a thousand times. Every two years. Always in January. Your bombing fit that pattern perfectly."

"That's right, it did. But when I read the paper and saw what had happened in Florida...something clicked." He waited, but she said nothing. "It's only been nine months since I was hurt, Hannah. Nine months."

"He's off his schedule." She put the glass on the table beside her. "That's obvious, Quinn. The team talked about it and we even had a shrink come in and discuss it with us. He told us what we already knew. That it was inevitable the bomber would begin to shorten the time span. The excitement's not lasting as long."

"I don't think that's it."

She raised her eyebrows and waited for him to continue.

"Let's just say I have a different perspective on this guy now...I'm in his head a bit more than I was before. And I definitely don't like what I see."

She understood instantly. *This* was why he'd called her. His intuition had picked up something she had missed.

She moved as if pulled by an unseen force to the window. "Tell me." She met his gaze and focused on it. "Tell me what you see, Quinn."

HANNAH DIDN'T WEAR PERFUME, but Quinn could smell her scent regardless. A natural fragrance clung to her skin, and catching a whiff of it, he completely lost track of what they were talking about before her gaze brought him back. Her stare was as intense and compelling as he'd ever seen it, and suddenly he felt as if she were trying to get inside his own mind and see for herself.

"He's smart," he began slowly. "And very clever. He likes to manipulate people, and he thinks he's got us buffaloed—"

"We know all that," she interrupted impatiently.

"Right, but there's one key element to his personality that's central. And I didn't see how important that was until I thought about it some more."

"And that is?"

"He's obsessive as hell. If this guy was a hand-washer, he'd never leave the bathroom."

She shook her head. "You've lost me—"

"He does everything the same way each time, Hannah. You're the one who discovered that, remember? He wraps the box the same way, he shapes the charge the same way, he uses the same materials…. Each time, the devices are identical, and that's how we know it's him. That's a sign of his obsessiveness." He paused. "Another sign of that is his timing. He plans his dates as carefully as he does everything else. It's of *paramount* importance to him that the bombings take place in January. That month probably represents an anniversary of something—his mother's birthday, when his dog died, hell, who knows? Maybe it was the first time he got laid. Whatever it is, it means everything to him. He wouldn't change it on a bet. This bombing doesn't fit that pattern."

She stood beside him without moving, her expression a curious mix he couldn't quite read. He could hear her brain clicking over the possibilities, though, and when she finally spoke, her voice sounded scared.

"I might have another piece that doesn't fit." She took a deep breath. "I found a wire. A *twisted* wire. Mr. Rogers always knotted his connections."

Quinn tensed. "Are you sure it was site-related?"

"The debris analysis came back inconclusive." She looked at him with troubled eyes. "I wasn't sure—the wire could have been part of the bomb or on-site before the detonation. The residue on the metal was minuscule."

He nodded. "I understand, but if you look at the larger picture... You found this wire, the timing is off, and there's another difference, too. A big difference. In New Orleans there were victims. In Destin, no one was hurt." He paused. "Guys like this don't go backward, Hannah. As sick as it is, we have to acknowledge that the deaths of those two kids would have juiced him good. He got more publicity, more attention, more everything... Killing the kids might have been an accident, but it's likely that the next bombing would have had victims, too."

"I just don't know, Quinn...." She pulled her bottom lip in and shook her head. "Even if all this is true, then where does it take us?"

Quinn had thought long and hard about how to say what he wanted to tell her, but now that the time was here, all he could do was blurt it out. "I believe it takes us in a whole different direction. I believe the Florida bombing was done by someone else."

She sucked in a sharp breath and started to question him, but he cut off her words, clamping his fingers on her arm. He felt as if he'd stuck his hand into a fire, but he didn't let go. He had to make sure she understood completely. "Someone who knows Mr. Rogers or knows what he does did Florida, Hannah. And whoever in the hell he is, he's just as dangerous, if not more so."

QUINN CONTINUED HIS argument until the sun slipped into the bayou, the dark green waters dousing the light but leaving the heat. They had moved to the porch in search of a breeze. Hannah pushed a strand of hair behind her ear and listened to Quinn repeat himself. His argument scared her to death, but she decided to play devil's advocate.

"I understand what you're saying, Quinn." She chose her words carefully. "But I'm not sure I completely agree with you."

He stood up, running his hands through his hair. "What's not to believe? I've laid it all out for you—"

"And I appreciate the help, but you haven't been in the office in months. You don't know the details of the case like you used to."

He stayed where he was for a moment, then he came to where she sat and pulled her to her feet. Her heart immediately began to pound as he took her back inside, down a short hall and into a bedroom.

But the room held no bed.

It was an office, with a desk and a filing cabinet and a computer. Papers were organized in neat piles with newspaper cuttings and printouts stapled beside them. On the walls he'd hung bulletin boards. They were covered with photographs and charts. Every piece of information had something to do with the bombings—his own, the previous ones and the latest incident in Florida. Some of the clippings she hadn't even seen herself. On the corner of his worktable was her latest report.

He dropped his fingers from her arm, but she could still feel his touch. Lifting her hand to where his had been, she turned in amazement to look at him. "What is this? Where did you get all—"

"I haven't been hiding out here, Hannah. I've been working. And I've kept track of everything."

"But how—"

"How is not important. What I've discovered means more."

"But who's your source?" She pointed to the edge of his desk. "These reports are *never* supposed to be copied, even inside the office, and you know that. Whoever did this for you should be fired immediately."

"Oh, for God's sake, Hannah! It doesn't matter, okay? The only thing you should care about is catching this guy."

She stopped and stared at him, drawing herself up

stiffly until he met her eyes. "That *is* the only thing I care about, Quinn. It's *all* I've worked on since you left."

His expression shifted in the low light from the desk lamp. "I understand," he said softly. "But I also know he's going to hit us again—and with two of them out there, the chances have doubled someone else is going to get killed."

"This is only a theory, Quinn. You can't be sure."

"I'd bet my life on it," he said. "Are you *that* sure I'm wrong?"

She couldn't answer the question.

Moving closer to where she stood, he lifted a finger and touched her cheek, shocking her into deeper stillness. "I'm only trying to help, Hannah. I don't want what happened to me to happen to…anyone else."

"I don't, either." She took a step away from him. "But I'm not sure this is the path to take."

"We've been tracking this guy for years and nothing has broken yet. If I'm right and there is a copycat, he could lead us to the real bomber. He *has* to know him. He wouldn't be able to get the details right unless he did. It's not inconceivable that they could even be working together. Criminal partners are unusual but they do exist—look at Bittaker and

Norris or Bianchi and Bunono. Don't forget Lake and Ng—''

She shook her head and argued. ''Those guys were serial killers. We've got a bomber—the profile is entirely different.''

''Maybe so, but it's not impossible, is it?''

''Impossible, no. Improbable, yes.''

''Men like this don't change, Hannah. Their routine is a part of them. They *can't* change it.'' His voice had stayed as it was in the hospital, low and whiskey-rough. It deepened even more as he spoke again. ''I'll bet you anything—you name it—the guy who did Florida is not the one who did New Orleans.''

Hannah turned and looked past Quinn to the boards behind him. One of them held a photograph of LaCroix carrying out one of the children. As it caught her gaze and held it, the pain of that night flowed over her again, as fresh and raw as it had been then.

Quinn came up behind her and put his hands on her back. The heat of his touch went straight through her clothing—she felt naked.

''I'm telling you the truth, Hannah.'' Turning her around to face him, he gripped her shoulders. ''And I can prove it to you. Spend tonight with me and I guarantee you'll be convinced by the time you leave.''

CHAPTER SEVEN

FOR TWO SECONDS HANNAH let herself fantasize, then she shook her head. "That's not going to happen, Quinn."

"I'll sleep on the couch, if that's what you're worried about. You can take the bed."

She immediately felt like a fool. A disappointed fool. To cover up, she said, "That issue never entered my mind. All I meant was that I can come back tomorrow and we can talk some more then."

"Why drive an hour just to turn around and do it again?" He flicked his hand at the cabin. "I know it's not the Ritz, but it doesn't make sense for you to leave, then return."

"And you know me better than to think I care about fancy sheets and a private bath."

"Then what's the problem?"

You are, she wanted to say. *You and your hot black eyes and your hands that never stop and your lips I want to taste.*

"I just don't believe it'd be a good idea." Thinking fast, she tilted her head toward the big house.

"Your renters really would have something to talk about then."

"And *you* know *me* better than to think I care what they talk about." He frowned at her. "Why the phony excuse, Hannah? Don't you want to hear what I have to say? Are you afraid I might be able to disprove some precious theory you've got?"

His challenge instantly set her teeth on edge, and she couldn't help but wonder if that had been his intention. She responded despite herself. "I don't have a theory, precious or otherwise. And if I did, I wouldn't be worried about your opinion of it. All I want is the truth. I want to solve this case and put this son of a bitch behind bars until past the end of time."

"Well, I can help you do that—stay here tonight and we can go over the case again."

She hesitated, unable to come up with another excuse. She'd die before she'd let him know how much she'd missed his touch, though. And besides that, she really could use some assistance. The case was starting to overwhelm her. Questioning her sanity, she finally agreed. "All right, I'll stay." Then, in an effort to reinforce her own resolve, she added, "But the door gets locked when it's time to go to bed. That part of our relationship is over, Quinn."

His eyes smoldered as he mocked her earlier

words. "That issue never even entered my mind…."

They stared at each other a moment longer. "I've got some fresh shrimp for dinner," he said after a bit. "I'll grill them outside." Starting toward the kitchen, he pointed over his shoulder toward the other side of the house. "There are shorts and T-shirts back there, if you want to get more comfortable while I start the fire."

Hannah waited until he left the room, then she let herself slump. Her legs felt like they had the last time she'd finished EXIT's mandatory physical fitness test. Weak. Shaky. With great effort, she pulled herself together and headed down the hall he'd indicated. She was crazy for agreeing to stay. Crazy. Crazy. Crazy.

She entered his bedroom. Surprisingly large, the room was lined with huge jalousied windows on three sides. Obviously a former porch, the area had been enclosed and converted into sleeping quarters. White gauze curtains fluttered in the breeze from a ceiling fan, but other than that, the place could have belonged to a monk. There were no photographs, no knickknacks, nothing of any personal nature at all.

Only a huge bed. With white sheets. And fluffy pillows.

She turned away quickly, but she wasn't fast enough. She'd seen two bodies entwined on the bed—her own and Quinn's—and nothing could erase the image. Fleeing the room, if not her thoughts, she went through the nearest door and found herself in his bathroom. As they did in the bedroom, the ceilings slanted high above her, and the all-white room was cool and dim. She went directly to the sink and splashed cold water over her face until she felt better. Grabbing a nearby towel, she blotted her forehead, then took a deep breath.

He'd used the towel before her and the scent of his soap filled her nostrils. Reacting like a little kid instead of a grown woman, she tried to hold her breath, but failed. She exhaled in a whoosh, then sucked in as much of the smell as she could hold. There was a sting at the back of her throat as she remembered everything they'd had together.

And everything they'd lost.

PULLING THE SHRIMP FROM the cooler outside, Quinn cursed and shook his head. That pretty little speech about keeping his distance was the biggest lie he'd told in a long time. From the minute Hannah had climbed out of the car and walked toward him, a sharp-edged desire had been slicing into him.

Their breakup had created a space in his heart that no one would ever be able to fill; the emptiness would always be his. He was well aware of that fact but seeing her in the flesh and experiencing the need to hold her and bring her close, to touch her skin and smell her hair…

God, his injuries hadn't killed him, but this damn well might.

Hannah opened the screen door and stepped outside to the porch. She'd traded her pants and jacket for a pair of his running shorts and an old T-shirt that read I'm a Bomb Technician. If You See Me Running, Try to Keep Up. He took one look, then turned away.

"There's beer in there, if you're interested." He pointed to a cooler at the end of the porch. "Cold drinks if you want something else."

He heard the lid lift, then fall again. A second later Hannah came to his side, holding a can of ginger ale. This time, he could smell his soap on her skin and it made him think about more things he shouldn't. He fought the pull of her nearness, but in the end, as he'd known all along that he would, he gave in to it. He asked, "How have you been, Hannah? Really?"

Her shoulders stiffened imperceptibly. She took a sip of the drink, then she faced him. "I've been fine," she said evenly. "Just fine. Things are going well."

"That's good," he said, holding up his end of the charade. "Everybody on the team doing okay?"

She nodded. "Mark's as obnoxious as ever and Bobby's working hard. He's a good boss, I guess."

"You guess?"

"He seems a little...remote sometimes. A little more quiet than he used to be." She shrugged. "He stays out of my way. That's all I care about."

"How about the other guys?"

"They're busy—we're all busy." She took another swallow from the can she held. "There's no shortage of bad guys with black powder and dynamite."

The silence between them grew, then stretched. After a while, Hannah looked over at him. "How about you?" she asked. "How have you been doing?"

He rearranged the coals beginning to glow at the bottom of the grill and wondered how to answer.

"Most of the time, I'm all right," he said finally. "But my therapy isn't going as quickly—or as smoothly—as I thought it would. Some days my leg doesn't want to work at all. I ignore it and press on, though. Everything else is okay, more or less." He tapped his chest and the scar beneath his shirt. "Other than looking like Frankenstein, that is..."

She smiled. "Frankenstein? I don't think so."

"You'd better wait till you see before you decide." He glanced at her. "It's not too pretty."

On the other side of the bayou the sun began to

ease down. The light painted red shadows over her
face that matched the fierceness in her voice. "Nothing about what happened was pretty." She stopped
abruptly, waited a moment, then spoke again. "Are
you coming back, Quinn?"

Her question surprised him—more for what she
didn't ask than for what she had. It wasn't "when,"
it was "if." He wondered if Barbara had told Hannah of their conversation.

"I want to," he answered honestly.

"But?"

"But…" He met her gaze unflinchingly and gave
voice to his fear. "I don't know if I can, Hannah. I
exercise daily and I'm making some headway, but I
should be stronger than I am."

She shook off his statements. "You always were
an impatient man. Give it some time."

"But I want to get back to work. Do something
productive."

She glanced over her shoulder, toward his office.
"It looks to me as if you've been pretty productive.
Right or wrong, no one has come up with what you
have."

He shrugged and they talked some more about the
case, Quinn doing his best to further explain his
theory. Finally he could no longer control his
thoughts from going to where they'd wanted to be
all along—on Hannah. He'd made a mistake asking

her to stay the night. Their past hung over the porch like a storm cloud waiting to burst. They were either going to fight...or make love.

Her hesitant voice broke into his thoughts. "About that wire, Quinn..."

He looked at her and nodded, curiously relieved she'd returned to the case. "Do you think I was wrong not to pursue that more?"

"Well, incongruent evidence is always important, Hannah. You know that as well as I do. But who's to say for certain? We all have to make judgment calls on things like that."

"I'm beginning to think I should have looked into it more. But when I told Bobby about it, he blew it off."

Quinn suddenly remembered his last conversation with the man who'd taken his place. Had Bobby lost all confidence in Hannah? It didn't seem possible, but who knew? "Bobby does things by the book, Hannah. He doesn't think out of the box. If it looks like a duck and quacks like a duck, he thinks it *is* a duck."

"And you don't?"

"You should know the answer to that," Quinn replied. "I've seen too much to make assumptions. You have to be skeptical. Otherwise, you're dead." He drained the beer sitting before him, then crumpled the can and dropped it to the table. After a bit, he leaned closer.

"Let me help you with this one, Hannah. I can work from here or come back to New Orleans—"

She was shaking her head before he'd finished. "You can't do that. You're still on leave."

"I'll ask Barroso for a reevaluation."

"It's too soon. You said yourself you weren't doing very well." Her eyes filled with a concern that looked genuine. "He might not clear you."

"Then I'll skip him and go directly to Bill Ford. He can give me a temporary clearance."

They discussed the possibility a little longer, but after a while it became obvious to Quinn that Hannah was reluctant. She didn't want him around.

He pushed back from the table, his chair scraping over the deck as a sudden breeze came up, the candle he'd placed between them earlier now flickering in the wind. Hannah's eyes glittered in the light, their color matching the deepest part of the flame. There was nothing Quinn could do but speak the truth.

"I've thought a lot about the way things ended, Hannah," he said quietly. "I don't know how it got so confused—"

She cut him off abruptly and stood, moving to the deck railing. "Forget about it," she said. "That's past history and it's over and done with. We've both moved on."

"Have we?"

She crossed her arms. Her stare didn't waver as she leaned against the wooden supports. "I don't know about you," she said, "but I definitely have."

The message was clear, and Quinn received it without changing his expression.

The relationship they'd shared was over.

He nodded once, then picked up the crushed beer can and flicked it into the trash container at the end of the deck. It hit the metal bottom and rang with the same finality Quinn now felt.

It was always good to know where you stood.

PLEADING EXHAUSTION AS soon as she could after dinner, Hannah escaped to the bathroom in the back of the house and turned on the shower. Ripping off Quinn's shorts and shirt, she stood beneath the stream of water without even waiting for it to heat. The icy shock took away her breath but did little to calm her mind. Everything between them had changed—and nothing had. They didn't have a real relationship…but the look in Quinn's eyes was as hot as it'd ever been.

She stayed under the spray until her skin began to wrinkle. Nine months had passed since Quinn had left New Orleans. None of the men she'd dated had gotten more than a kiss on the cheek. Hannah stepped outside the shower and began to towel off. She missed being held, being kissed, being loved... The physical aspect of their relationship had always been of paramount importance to them both. In fact, it'd been more like a need than a desire. She wondered, and not for the first time, if that had been the only glue holding them together.

She slipped into one of Quinn's clean T-shirts, then combed out her hair, the strands hanging down her back, wet and heavy. Turning off the bathroom light, she went into the bedroom, her way lit by the moonlight pouring in through the open windows. She paused by one and looked outside. The bayou stretched before her like a ribbon of white silk, the surface rippling gently. The serenity of the scene should have made her feel peaceful and calm, but all it did was make her realize how lonely her life had become since Quinn had left New Orleans.

When he knocked on the door and opened it, she turned in surprise, her mouth going dry.

"I wanted to make sure you were okay," he said. "You seemed anxious to end the evening. Is everything all right?"

"I'm fine," she lied. "Just...a little tired, I guess. The drive out and everything..." Her voice trailed off. He wore a pair of loose pants tied with a string at the waist and nothing else. Only her heart could hear the warning that sounded deep inside her. *Tell him to leave,* it said. *You'll be hurt again, and the second time is always worse than the first.*

He waited for her to say something more, but Hannah couldn't. She was suddenly paralyzed by a desire that left her unable to speak. Only when her eyes fell to his bare chest was the silence broken. She sucked in her breath without thinking, a sharp gasp that she cut off too late.

"I warned you," he said softly.

Hannah slowly crossed the room, stopping at the edge of the bed as her eyes took in the scar on his chest. It was wicked-looking and deep, a ragged line that bisected the width of his upper body. In the hospital he'd been bandaged and she'd never seen it.

She lifted her gaze to his. "Does it hurt?"

"I know it's there, but the actual pain is gone."

"I had no idea…"

He smiled slightly. "Neither did I. The first time I saw it in the mirror I even scared myself." He patted his thigh. "Wait till you see the rest of it. The doc actually did a fair job stitching my chest compared to my leg."

Under the power of something other than good sense, Hannah closed the distance between them and put her hand on Quinn's chest. His skin was warm and she could feel his heart beating beneath the twisting line. Without thinking about what she was doing, she bent her head and kissed the awful scar.

THE TOUCH OF HANNAH'S LIPS against his skin was all it took.

Quinn lifted her face and brought her mouth to his, wrapping his arms around her body and clutching her closer. There was nothing tentative about the kiss they shared. She wanted him as badly as he wanted her. Quinn didn't know what he would have done if he'd sensed anything different. He deepened the kiss, edging his tongue past her lips. Her mouth tasted just as he remembered it, sweet and soft.

He'd dreamed this scene so many times, he wasn't sure it was actually happening. He moved down the line of her jaw and breathed in her clean, fresh scent, reassuring himself he was awake. The curves beneath his hands were real, her wet hair too silky to be anything else. He tangled his hands in it and pulled her head back, exposing her throat, his mouth tracing a path up and down her neck. She moaned in response, a sound that evoked a new rise of desire inside him.

After a lifetime, he eased back. Despite all the indications, he still had to hear her say this was what she wanted. He had to give her a chance to back out.

"Hannah..." Her name came out a whisper. "Are you sure—"

She put her finger over his lips and stopped his words. "Don't ask me that." Her eyes gleamed in the moonlight. "If you ask me that question, I'll have to answer it and I don't want to do that right now. All I want...is you."

He nodded once, then kissing again, they moved in unison toward the edge of the bed. A moment later, they were tangled in the sheets.

HANNAH KNEW SHE'D REGRET her actions in the morning, but the thought came and went in a haze. Quinn's hands were everywhere at once, stroking her, touching her, loving her as no one else's could. In what was left of her consciousness, she tried to correct herself—this wasn't love. It was lust, it was desire, it was sexual gratification, but it wasn't love.

She didn't care.

Her body took over, any last-minute considerations evaporating in the heat that was building between them. He continued to kiss her, but when he got to her shoulders, the kisses turned into bites, tiny nips that sent sparks racing across her skin.

Greedy for the feel of him, she slid her hands over his bare skin, the lines and angles of his body as familiar to her as her own. Underneath her fingers, there *were* differences, though. The ropy scar covering his chest had been shocking, but his leg, as he'd warned, was even worse. She traced the rough lines with her mouth and tried not to cry. He was a wounded man with the scars to show for it. Just as she had earlier, she wondered if he'd changed inside as well. Something told her he may very well have, but when his mouth and tongue dropped lower, she forgot her question.

Time slowed as Hannah lay in the knotted sheets and gave herself over to Quinn. Everywhere he touched her, she felt a corresponding heat deep inside her. Finally that heat—and the need it created—grew until she could think of nothing else. She clutched his back and pulled him to her. He entered her as if he'd never left, the rhythm between them swiftly building to a climax.

The thought came to her that she should remember this very second, that she should freeze it into her brain, but that was lost in what followed.

And so was she.

THE SECOND TIME THEY went slower.

Cradling Hannah in the crook of his arm, Quinn pressed his mouth against hers and slipped his tongue inside. She groaned, low in her throat, and the sound of that, along with all the memories it brought, was more than enough to arouse him again.

She wrapped her arms around his neck and clung

tightly, murmuring against his chest. Just as it had earlier, when he'd first pulled her into his arms, the old sensation of needing her, wanting her, having to have her, entered Quinn's bloodstream with a fierceness that surprised him. He'd forgotten the sensation, but it came back to him with dizzying speed. The connection between them was still there...and it probably always would be.

Skimming his hands down the curve of her back, Quinn quickly remembered everything else, as well. The smoothness of her skin, the strength of her body, the subtle ways she led his touch. Arching beneath him, she raised herself to meet his hand as it curved around her hip. He moved his fingers between her legs, and once again she began to moan. He lost track after that. He forgot himself and forgot their problems, nothing mattering to him any longer but the friction between them and the rising heat of his desire.

In their profession, the luxury of second chances didn't exist. Holding Hannah in his arms, loving her once more, Quinn was amazed at what had happened between them. He felt more in love with Hannah than ever before, and something told him she felt the same.

He vowed at once not to let the opportunity slip by.

He woke up in the middle of the night, Hannah's

head heavy against his arm. Tucked into the hollow of his chest, she had her hand spread protectively over his scar. His heart swelled with an extra beat, then he covered her fingers with his and went back to sleep.

In the morning, they'd start over.

THE SUNLIGHT LAY IN stripes across the bedroom floor when Hannah opened her eyes the next morning. It was almost noon. The sheets were wrinkled and scented with Quinn's soap, but other than that, there was no evidence Quinn had even been there. For a second, she wondered if she had fantasized the whole episode; it wouldn't have been the first time. She might have been able to convince herself that was the case, except her body told her otherwise.

Besides, Hannah wasn't the kind of woman who was good at pretending. She'd done exactly what she'd wanted to last night and faking any other response, if only to herself, wasn't something she could do.

She'd wanted Quinn to make love to her and he had. That had been it. No strings, she told herself. No commitments. No emotional attachments, which meant no chance for hurt. She'd tell him that, then she'd take the situation back to where it should have stayed. She rehearsed what she wanted to say until the words sounded convincing, then she swung her legs out of the bed and padded across the floor to the bathroom.

Ten minutes later she was dressed in the suit she'd worn the day before, her hair tamed by a rubber band she found in one of Quinn's drawers. When she opened the bedroom door, a familiar scent came down the hall. Quinn added as much chicory as he did coffee to what he brewed—the smell was rich and dark. It led her into the kitchen, then out to the porch.

He was sitting in one of the patio chairs with his feet on the railing. He looked up as the screen door squeaked and she stepped outside.

His eyes roved over her face and then her suit. "Good morning," he said.

She wanted to appear calm and untouched by what had happened between them, but the way Quinn looked, sitting there with his expression relaxed and his shirt open, had Hannah struggling, the words she'd practiced suddenly fleeing her mind. What was wrong with her? Where had her resolve gone? She returned his greeting, and he pointed toward a mug.

"I poured you a cup. Black, no sugar."

She picked up the sturdy white mug, then brushed past him to take the chair on the other side. She managed one step before he captured her hand, but it was his gaze, not his grip, that kept her from moving on. She felt the intensity of his eyes all the way down to her toes. "Hannah—"

"Don't say it." She pulled her fingers away and sat down.

"You don't even know what I was about to—"

"Yes, I do." She sipped from the mug, then put it down on the table beside her chair. "You were going to say something about what happened between us last night, and I don't want to talk about it. I don't want to analyze it."

"What do you want to do?" He paused, a half-teasing glint lightening his eyes. "Ignore the whole event?"

"That would work for me."

As her answer registered, his smile evaporated. Disbelief, then confusion replaced it. "Well, it won't work for me. Not by a long shot."

He straightened and faced her, spreading his hands on either side of her thighs. His touch instantly took her back to the bedroom. "Last night was too important to dismiss. I don't want to act like it didn't happen. I can't."

"People do that all the time and then ignore the consequences."

"Some people might," he said. "But not me. And not you, either."

Taking a deep breath, she faced him squarely and

gave him her speech. "Look, Quinn, we're two consenting adults. We're not married and not involved with anyone else. What we did wasn't illegal or hurtful to anyone. I wanted it and you wanted it. I suggest we leave the conversation at that."

"That's not possible."

"Why?"

His voice turned even angrier. "Because we didn't just shake hands, dammit! We made love to each other for hours and that means something—"

"You bet it does," she said suddenly. "It means we were fools who let our good sense abandon us. That's all."

"That's all?" he repeated incredulously.

She nodded and look him straight in the eye. "That's all."

A tinny ringing suddenly sounded from inside the cabin. Quinn groaned in disgust at the noise, then threw up his hands. "I don't have a cell phone—if that's one going off, it's yours."

She jumped from the chair and ran inside to her purse. Dumping the contents, she found the phone just as the sound stopped. She flipped it open, but before she could even punch out the commands to get the caller's number, the unit began to ring again. She answered it quickly. "Crosby here."

"And where exactly is *here?*"

Mark Baker's voice took her by surprise, even

though it shouldn't have. She recovered quickly. "None of your business. What's up?"

"I'll answer your question if you'll reveal your secret location. Your mother refused to share it when I called your house."

Hannah heard the screen door open behind her. Quinn had come into the room. "Cut the baloney, Mark, and tell me what you want."

"Why, you, of course, Hannah. You. Always."

"I'm going to hang up unless you say something important in the next three seconds. One, two—"

"I can't find the report you requested on the Mississippi bombing. It's gone."

She thought of the copies sitting on Quinn's desk. There was no way she could explain to Mark how she'd come up with a copy of it, even if Quinn did have one. For the good of the team, she should turn in the leak—but she wouldn't and she knew it. "What do you mean, the report is gone?"

"It's not in the old file. The folder is empty. It is no longer available. Someone has taken it. I don't know what the hell happened to it, but it's not where it's supposed to be." He paused. "It's gone."

"Look again."

"I did."

"Then look again again. It's got to be there. Files don't walk away by themselves."

"I'm aware of that fact. I just thought you might like to know I *am* working on the situation."

"That's fine," she said impatiently. "Thanks a lot." She started to hang up, but his voice stopped her.

"You might like to know something else, too. Something about Florida."

Her pulse quickened. "What about Florida?"

"The SWAT commander wants to talk to you. She's come up with a possible match to our Mr. Rogers."

Shocked by his words, she reacted with irritation. "God, Mark, why didn't you tell me this first?"

"I like to save the best till last."

"Who is it?"

"I don't know. The commander wanted to talk to you about it, not me. She said you ought to catch the next flight out, though."

She cursed as Mark's words registered. If she'd brought her files and evidence kits with her, she could have left from St. Martin and driven to Florida. As it was, she'd have to go back to New Orleans, pack up everything, then leave from there. Valuable time would be wasted, but she didn't have a choice. "Call the commander back and tell her I'll be in touch as soon as I can. I have to come in and get my things, then I'll head straight for the airport."

"Okay," he said, "but you gotta tell me where you are as payment."

She ignored him. "Is there anything else?"

He waited a minute. "There's always something else, Hannah. Always and forever…"

She snapped the phone shut, Mark's voice still sounding in her ear as she turned to look at Quinn. "I have to leave. Something's come up in Florida."

"They got a suspect?"

"I'm not sure," she hedged. "Maybe, maybe not. I need to get out of here and find out."

"And our conversation?"

"Our conversation is over." Avoiding his eyes, she began to pick up the contents of her purse and stuff them back where they belonged. "There's nothing else we need to discuss. If I have any questions about your theory, I'll call." She slung her bag over her shoulder, then straightened up.

His gaze locked on hers and her heart constricted inside her chest. It physically hurt—she had to stop herself from raising her hand to the aching spot.

"That's it, Hannah? You'll call?"

She didn't answer because she couldn't. She'd lied to herself and to Quinn when she'd said sleeping with him wouldn't hurt anyone.

It'd hurt *her*. With a cut so deep and painful she wasn't sure she'd ever be able to recover. She'd been an idiot for coming here.

She made a promise then and there that making love with Quinn wouldn't happen again. She would not allow herself to become a victim of her own foolishness or of Quinn's. All at once, she remembered the vow she'd made the day of the bombing. Up and down, in and out. He'd been able to twist her every way possible. They'd fallen into the same old pattern and she hadn't even thought about it until now.

She couldn't let that cycle start all over again. If she did, she was doomed.

She met his disbelieving eyes. "That's it," she said tightly. "I'll call." She turned and went outside, the door banging hard behind her.

CHAPTER EIGHT

QUINN WALKED OUTSIDE to the front porch. A flash of red told him when Hannah's car connected with the main highway, then the bayou fell silent again, the caw of a crow the only sound to infiltrate the quiet.

He'd been a fool. A complete and utter fool.

What had made him think that making love with Hannah could heal the wounds between them, the wounds that continued to keep them apart? Sitting on the deck, staring at the water and waiting for her to wake that morning, he'd let all the possibilities run through his head. He'd assumed their old problems were still there, but somehow they'd deal with them. Somehow...

How could he have been so stupid?

He stomped back inside and straight through to the porch, where he grabbed the hoe propped by the door. Forty minutes later he'd cleared the garden of anything resembling a weed and had a new plot ready for seeding. Limping across the freshly turned dirt, he gritted his teeth, pain throbbing through his thigh. Most men would have quit long before the aching had reached this point, but Quinn was thankful for it. The hot stabs took his mind from the other ache, the one that was building inside his heart.

But the distraction didn't last long. Walking outside to his porch after he'd cleaned up, a glass of iced tea in his hand, Quinn had to work hard—again—to divert his mind from his mistake. He chose to focus on Hannah's telephone conversation. He'd heard only snatches of it, but clearly she'd been talking to Mark Baker. She'd never liked Baker, and frankly, Quinn hadn't, either. Despite that fact, they'd developed a casual friendship, simply because Baker had visited the hospital so often.

But why had Baker come by so frequently? Why had he been so friendly? Quinn had asked him those questions once and he'd shrugged. Then he'd said something surprising.

"I had a brother on a squad in Massachusetts. He ran into a situation like yours...but he wasn't as lucky. I knew how much it meant to him to know that the team still cared. Right before he died, he told me their visits were the only thing that had kept him alive that long...."

Quinn had accepted the explanation, then forgotten about it. In retrospect, sipping his tea, he decided Baker's explanation could have been made up, a handy excuse to account for his presence. Offhand,

Quinn couldn't think of any other reason the man would want to visit him, but that didn't necessarily mean anything sinister. Maybe he'd wanted to stay in touch. Maybe there was a nice guy under all the bravado. Maybe Baker's story had been the truth and he'd really thought he could comfort Quinn somehow.

Quinn sat down on the steps and mopped his face with his shirt, the bayou's humidity already over-powering the cool shower he'd just taken. That was a lot of maybes to consider. Could any of them be the truth?

He took a deep gulp of tea, then out of nowhere, another possibility came into his mind. He wondered why he'd never considered it before.

Maybe, just maybe, there had been someone else at the hospital Baker had wanted to comfort. Some-one like Hannah…

Jolie had told Quinn that as soon as he'd left town, Mark had put the moves on Hannah. Quinn had dismissed the news at the time, but now he wondered.

And then he wondered some more.

Baker was a good-looking guy, yet as far as Quinn could tell, Hannah had never given him any kind of encouragement. Her rejection must have stung a man who was usually a hit with the ladies. How long had he been carrying the torch? Quinn wondered. Had Baker's interest in Hannah started after Quinn's accident…or had it been there all along, even before the accident?

Which had come first?

The question opened a floodgate, and a wave of more possibilities followed. The obvious conclusion plagued Quinn until he couldn't take it any longer. Picking up the phone, he did what he should have done when he'd first learned of the Florida bombing. Then he made one more call.

Half an hour later he was on the road.

HANNAH TRIED LENA A DOZEN times between St. Martin and New Orleans, but the SWAT team commander was out. Finally, she managed to locate Lena's second-in-command, a man named Bradley Thompson. He confirmed Mark Baker's information. They did indeed have a target—a local man Lena had uncovered. He didn't know more than that so Hannah asked him to tell Lena she would be there on the first flight out. Thompson's deep voice reassured her there was no hurry—the man in question wasn't going anywhere.

An hour later, sliding into her parking spot at headquarters, Hannah headed straight for her office and began to gather her things, stopping only to look for the files Mark had said he couldn't find. The search proved to be a frustrating waste of time. To top things off, Mark wasn't around and no one had seen him all day.

By the time she left the office, it was almost three. Hannah called her mother from the car, her voice clipped.

"I've got to go to Florida, Ma. Could you throw some things into my black bag? I'm on my way home, and if you could have my suitcase packed, it'd really save me some time."

"Did you see him?"

Hannah didn't need to ask her mother who she meant. "Yeah, Ma. I saw him. Can you—"

"When you didn't come home, I figured dark must have caught you and you decided to stay. For safety's sake, of course."

"Of course," Hannah echoed. "Look, Ma, I really need that suitcase—"

"How is he?"

Incredible. Unbelievable. Fantastic. Too sexy to even think about in public.

Between her anxiousness to get out of town and her craziness with Quinn, Hannah wanted to scream the answer at her mother. But she didn't. "He's lost some weight and he looks a little older. But basically he's okay. We had a very productive discussion. He realized something about the case that I hadn't considered. He wanted to talk to me about it."

"Is that all he's realized?"

"What do you mean?"

"You know what I mean," Barbara said sharply. "Did you two work out your problems or are you still pretending you don't love each other?"

"We're not pretending anything, Ma. Nothing's changed. Quinn doesn't love me and I don't love him. That part of our relationship is over."

"If that's the case, then why are you so upset?"

"Who says I'm upset?"

"I've been your mother for thirty-three years, Hannah. I can tell by your voice you're upset."

"You're wrong."

"No, ma'am, *you're* wrong. You're wrong *and* you're lying. To me and to yourself."

Swinging off the freeway, Hannah held back a groan. She was almost home. "Look, Ma, I just called to ask for your help. I need that—"

Her mother interrupted her. "Your bag's ready, Hannah. I was packing while we were talking. I *can* do more than one thing at a time, you know."

With that, Barbara hung up, and five minutes later, Hannah pulled into her driveway. Her mother was standing outside with the suitcase and a plastic bag of cookies.

Ignoring the look in her mother's eyes, Hannah kissed her, grabbed the bag and suitcase, then jumped back in the car and took off. Barbara's interrogation skills beat every cop's Hannah knew.

And to make matters worse, her questions stuck with Hannah, following her all the way to Florida. By the time the plane landed, Hannah was exhausted from asking herself the same things. Why on earth had she slept with Quinn? What had she been thinking? Walking into the Destin terminal, she knew she'd satisfied a momentary desire, but in the process she'd created a much bigger problem.

She came out of her thoughts to witness the reunion of a woman from her flight and the man who'd obviously been waiting for her. She hugged him and the baby he held. Their happiness was palatable. Hannah tried to ignore it, but couldn't.

She hailed the first cab she saw and gave the driver the address of the SWAT team's office. It was late but someone was always there.

Work had healed her wounds before. It'd heal her now as well.

"DO YOU HAVE A VISUAL, Jason? Talk to me. What do you see?"

As Hannah entered the SWAT team's command-and-control vehicle, Lena turned and waved her inside, continuing her conversation at the same time. Thompson had told Hannah a domestic disturbance had escalated into a standoff and negotiations were just beginning. No one had any idea how long it could take. After contacting Lena, he'd been instructed to send Hannah out to her, explaining that she might be tied up for hours.

The commander wore a headset with a tiny microphone and corresponding earpieces and was obviously talking to an officer already deployed.

Hannah acknowledged Lena, then realized there was another officer with her—a big man with white hair and an imposing attitude. Nodding at him as well, Hannah sat down on a bench built into the wall. The converted RV held almost as much equipment as the EXIT vehicles. Some of the tools—the mirrors and hooks—took Hannah back to her days as a firefighter. She'd tried to avoid SWAT missions because they always left her shaken and breathless. EXIT was completely different and that's why she'd applied. She knew what to expect from bombs; SWAT dealt with people.

Crazy people.

Placing her fingers against her earpiece, Lena listened and nodded. "All right," she said finally. "As far as we know, the perp has no weapons, no hostages, nothing. We're going to stay in place and wait him out." She flashed a look toward the guy in the back and he nodded once. "Beck thinks that's the best route and so do I. Keep a sharp eye but settle in. We're gonna be here for a while."

Lena swiveled her chair to face Hannah, pulling off her receiver as she spoke. "I'm sorry I had to drag you out here to talk, but this could take all night.'' She glanced at her watch and grimaced. ''Or what's left of it,'' she added.

''Let's hope it does.'' The officer in the back came forward. He reminded Hannah of a Viking. ''The longer he talks to us, the better our chances.''

Lena nodded, then introduced Hannah to Beck Winters, the team's senior negotiator. He'd left the safety of a desk job and returned to his first love, Lena explained. ''He was driving everyone in the office nuts,'' she said with a grin. ''When he started negotiating with the guy from the bakery, we knew it was time to get him back in the field.''

''He wasn't bringing the right kind of doughnuts! We needed more glazed and fewer cake.'' He shot Hannah a look of mock disgust. ''Who eats cake doughnuts, anyway?''

''I agree,'' Hannah answered seriously. ''They're not nearly as fattening. Why eat that when you could have one with all that extra sugar and calories?''

The humor might have seemed inappropriate considering what was going on, but they each understood. Downtime in a situations like this was important. To be sharp when they had to, they needed to relax, if only for a few seconds.

Lena cut the joking off quicker than usual, though, her expression becoming serious as she turned to Hannah. ''I'm glad you could get here so fast. We got a lead on a guy I think you need to look into.''

"He's a nut.'' Beck poured a cup of coffee from a thermos and offered it to Hannah. She shook her head and he began to sip from the mug. "A dangerous nut.''

Lena took over. "His name is Bob Inlandson, but everyone calls him Brother Bob.''

Hannah raised an eyebrow.

"He's an ordained minister. He preaches to his flock over the radio—he doesn't have a real church per se. His recording studio is out in the middle of the woods, off Choctawhatchee Bay.''

Hannah leaned back on the bench. "A preacher?''

Lena rocked her hand. "There's some controversy about the legitimacy of his ordination but there's no question of his beliefs. Everyone who's ever heard him knows exactly where he's coming from.''

"And that is?'' Hannah asked.

"Keep 'em barefoot and pregnant. The world has no place for working mothers.'' Beck blew on his coffee, then looked at her. "If you have kids, stay home.''

"So he hates day-care centers,'' Hannah said slowly.

Lena nodded. "After you left, I ran a general database search on misdemeanors in Santa Rosa,

Okaloosa and Walton counties. Our information officer had some free time so I had her analyze the
data. She recognized Inlandson's name and it
clicked for me, too, because I can pick up his radio
program out where I live. DPD arrested him a few
years back for organizing a protest at a day-care
center. He had some women carrying signs and
making pests of themselves outside a place in Fort
Walton.''

Disappointed, Hannah didn't want to make light
of what Lena had found, but EXIT had already
checked out anyone with priors that might be relevant. If Brother Bob had been a real possibility, he
would have been registered in the federal system.

''Look, I really appreciate the help—you don't
know how much—but we already queried the federal and local systems.''

''I assumed as much, but I know something about
this guy that the database doesn't. I heard him mention it once on his show.''

''And that is?''

''He's an ex-Navy Master Blaster,'' Lena said. ''I
called NAVSCOLEOD and they verified it.''

''Whoa....'' Hannah's eyebrows shot up and so
did her interest.

NAVSCOLEOD—the Naval school—was fa-
mous for the explosive ordnance disposal techs it
produced. There was one instructor for every five

students, and damn few of them made it all the way to the top. It took years of study and years of experience for a student to earn the stars above his "crab," the insignia of the branch.

The school was located at Eglin, the air force base just off Choctawhatchee Bay.

"Has he got any kind of sheet other than the protest?" Hannah asked.

"No." Lena shook her head. "He's pure as the driven snow."

"But he's a nutcase, and he has access to military explosives and he knows how to use them." Hannah shook her head. "Oh, boy…"

The three of them sat quietly and absorbed the implications. When the radio crackled to life, Hannah jumped.

"L1 to Base."

Lena snatched up her headset and answered the call. Listening for a moment, she nodded to herself. "Hang tight, L1." She looked at Beck and jerked her head toward his station at the back of the RV. "Jason thinks the perp might be ready to talk. Get on and see what's happening."

The negotiator moved quickly, the tension in the RV going up a notch. "I'm sorry," Lena said to Hannah, "but things are probably going to get tricky now. You can stay, but if you want to leave, then you'd better do it now. Otherwise you're here for the duration. We can't risk a departure if we start to negotiate.''

Hannah had enough tension in her life without borrowing any from the SWAT team. "I'm going back to my hotel to make some calls. We'll want to talk to this guy ASAP."

"He's all yours," Lena replied. "The radio station is right past the Mid Bay Bridge. Take 98 going east, then left on the bridge. You can't miss it—he's got a huge sign shaped like the sun and the letters are lit all day. Golden Light Ministries. Let me know what you find out."

"I will," Hannah said. "And I really appreciate everything—"

Acknowledging Hannah's thanks with a wave, Lena pressed her fingers against her ear and returned to her job, speaking into her headset before Hannah could step outside. "Okay now, let's watch this guy, everyone. Take it slow and easy. There's no hurry...."

AFTER A QUICK STOP at the twenty-four hour Wal-Mart to pick up some essentials her mother hadn't packed, Hannah drove back to the motel where she'd stayed the first time. It was almost 4:00 a.m. She checked in, then headed directly to her room, carrying the plastic bags, having left her suitcase in the car. She'd need to call the office and take care of the paperwork before contacting Brother Bob. If there was any chance he was Mr. Rogers, she wanted to make sure this went down according to the book. She'd call the office first and get that going, then she'd crash for a few hours, if her brain would let her. Thoughts of Quinn refused to leave her alone so she wasn't sure if she could even sleep given the chance. Just as she put the key in the door, a voice spoke from behind her.

"Now, that's what I call traveling light…."

Hannah turned to face Mark Baker. He nodded toward her purchases. "I think I'll start packing my clothes in bags like that. Very chic."

Too surprised to bother with niceties, she spoke with irritation. "What are you doing here?"

"I was already here when I called you. I want to help."

Hannah set down her briefcase and dropped the bags to the sidewalk. He hadn't even been able to locate a simple file, but here he was. She was beginning to suspect Mark's best effort to "help" her would be to "help" her out of her clothes. Then another possibility came to her.

"Did Bobby think I needed backup?" It was impossible to keep the defensiveness from her voice.

"I didn't ask him," Mark answered. "He left for vacation yesterday, remember?"

"Well, I appreciate your concern," she said.

"But you've wasted your time coming to Destin. I've got this one under control."

"There's a suspect out there and you've got to go talk to him. You wanna do that alone?"

He had a good point, but Mark was the last person she'd want going with her to see Brother Bob. Something told her he wouldn't know how to question a preacher. "Alone is how I planned to do it," she said. "I've handled suspects by myself before."

"Not like this," he countered. "You and I both know Mr. Rogers isn't the kind of perp that would take kindly to questions." Mark's voice went serious. "This guy is scary, Hannah. I don't think you should go without someone else along."

"She won't. I can go with her."

They both turned quickly, Hannah going into shock at the appearance of the man behind her. She couldn't believe her eyes, but it was her heart that took the impact.

"Quinn!" Her pulse leapt. "What in the hell are *you* doing here?"

Ignoring Hannah, he looked at Mark. "You working this case, too?"

The tech smiled easily. "I work 'em all, Chief. You know me. Gotta be where the action is."

Hannah let her eyes go from Quinn's face to Mark's, then back again. What was going on? She could almost see the strain between the two men.

"What are you doing here?" She repeated her question to Quinn.

His eyes were fastened on hers, their intensity a contrast to the casual tone in his voice. All at once, the only thing she could think of was the night they'd shared. Flashes of it came quickly to her mind—her hand against his scar, his teeth upon her neck, the tangled sheets and hoarse sighs.

"I heard this was a nice place," he said. "I thought it might do me some good to get away for a while so I hopped in the car and drove over."

She forced herself to focus. "And you just happened to decide now was the time to do that?"

"Seemed like a good idea. Why not?" he asked.

Hannah started to tell him why not, but Mark broke into the conversation. He sent Quinn a curious look, then said, "I'm going back to my room to read some reports. Call me later and brief me, Hannah. Whenever you're ready, I'm ready."

Without another word, he went into a room three doors down. She looked at Quinn. "I don't know what you think you're doing, but you're still on medical leave. You shouldn't be here. You could get canned for this—"

He tilted his head to her room. "Can we go inside and talk?"

She hesitated, then realized she didn't have a choice. They couldn't very well stand outside on the sidewalk and finish this discussion. Picking up her things, she turned the key she'd left in the lock and pushed the door open with her foot. Quinn followed.

The room was chilly and dark, the air conditioner humming softly. Dropping her bags on top of the bedspread, she turned to speak. Quinn was standing right behind her, and for a second she thought he was going to embrace her. Her heart thumped...then tumbled as she remembered her vow and took a step backward, increasing the space between them. "Why are you here?"

"I came to help you."

"You don't work for EXIT now, Quinn, and I don't need your help. I appreciate the input you gave me, but I can handle this one on my own."

"It's not a question of whether you're able or not." He closed the gap between them. "You can do the job, Hannah. But you can use my help, too."

"Not officially, I can't."

"I called Washington. Bill Ford gave me a temporary okay, pending Barroso's permanent release."

"A temporary okay—" Her voice reflected her surprise, then she remembered who she was dealing with. Ford had joined the team five years before Quinn, but they'd been friends even before that. It would have been a simple task for him to get Ford on his side. "Does Bobby know about this?"

"Bobby's on vacation this week. That's why I called D.C."

His persistence in the matter was something she hadn't expected, either, but Hannah understood as the pieces clicked into place. He wanted to prove his theory. That's why he'd called her out to the bayou. That's why he'd wanted to talk to her about the timing issue. That's why he'd asked her to spend the night. Had making love to her been part of his plan or had that just happened?

The question rocked her. So much so she couldn't face it right now. She shook her head wearily. "I'm tired. I have to call the office, then I'm shutting it down. I want a bath, then something to eat, then sleep. If you're still here when I wake up, we'll talk about it." She pointed to the door behind him. "I'd like you to leave now."

"That's fine. If you change your mind and want to discuss it before then—" he tilted his head toward the wall behind the bed "—I'm right next door. Knock twice and I'll come over."

He left her more confused than ever.

QUINN WAITED FOR HANNAH in the hotel's coffee shop. She'd called him after catching a few hours' sleep and told him to meet her there. He had the feeling she didn't want him back in her room and he understood completely. He didn't want to be there, either. The temptation to pull her down to the bed and continue where they'd left off was too powerful for him to resist.

He shouldn't have come.

But the more he'd thought about their conversation, and Mark Baker's visits to his hospital room, the more uncomfortable Quinn had become. Leaving Hannah to deal with this on her own simply hadn't been an option. Talking to Bill Ford, Quinn had kept his theories to himself but still managed to get what he wanted. In the end, it didn't matter, anyway. If he thought it would help his own career, Ford would have given Quinn permission to jump off the Sunshine Bridge wearing a pink tutu and a cowboy hat.

When Hannah came into the cheerful yellow dining room a few minutes later, Quinn's mind blanked. She wore a blue sweater that made her eyes glow and a pair of jeans that fit just right. His gut tightened.

She sat down and he waved to the waitress to distract himself. The woman took Hannah's order and left before either of them said a word.

Hannah shook out her napkin, put it over her lap and got straight to the point. "I don't know what you're doing here, Quinn, but you can't stay. You're well aware of why, so I'm not even going into it."

"I'm well aware of quite a few things," he answered slowly. "Some of which seem to have escaped your notice."

"What does that mean?"

He leaned closer, his elbows on the table. "Where's Baker this morning?"

A momentary flash of confusion crossed her face. "I sent him to Pensacola on an errand, then I told him to go back to New Orleans. I don't want him around."

"I don't, either," Quinn said, "but I have a feeling our reasons are different."

"He's a pain," Hannah said. "He'd be more trouble than help when I question this suspect. But what's this got to do with anything? Why do you care if he's here or not?"

Quinn spoke bluntly. "I'm suspicious of him, Hannah. Someone like Baker would have the ability to copycat Mr. Rogers."

Her mouth actually dropped open. It stayed that way until the waitress brought their coffee and their plates. When the woman walked away, Hannah spoke. "Are you crazy? You think Mark Baker could be behind this bombing?"

"I believe it's something we should consider."

She sat motionless and stared at him, her breakfast cooling on the table between them. "What on earth made you come up with this?"

Quinn raised his hand and ticked the items off

with his fingers. "One, he has access. Two, he has ability. Three, he has motive."

"Access to the materials, I understand. Ability to make the bombs, I might agree. Motivation..." She shook her head and stared at him. "What could possibly motivate Mark Baker to bomb a day-care center?"

Quinn gave it to her in one word. "You."

Her eyes rounded. "Me? What the hell—" Realizing her voice had risen, she lowered it. "What are you saying, Quinn? I don't understand."

"I'm not sure I do, either, but I started thinking about it after you left. The pieces fell in place a little too conveniently for me to ignore. I had to come here and tell you."

"You're crazy."

"Listen to me, Hannah! He's always been after you. Even before my accident, his interest in you was no secret. That hasn't changed, has it?"

"No, but—"

"When was the last time he asked you out?"

"Last week."

Quinn held out his hands.

"But I'm still turning him down."

"All the more reason to try harder."

"How on earth can you link that to a bombing? That's a little extreme—"

"It brought you together, didn't it?" Not waiting

for an answer, Quinn continued. "He came down here 'to help.' He's chasing everything from missing files to missing people for you. If I hadn't shown up last night, I have no doubt he'd be sitting here with you instead of me. It's a way—and a damn good one—to bring the two of you closer together." He stopped and took a deep breath. "Not to mention, getting the competition—and that would be *me*—out of the way."

She looked at him with a stunned expression, her cheeks losing their color. Quinn pressed forward.

"Mark Baker's sharp. Behind the bravado and fast talk, he's got a brain. Even if he didn't want me dead, he's got a good plan. What better way to impress you than to help you with this case? He could find something important about the bombing— something no one had seen before but that he conveniently discovered. Wouldn't that make you happy? Wouldn't you be grateful?" Quinn paused. "At least you'd go out with him to celebrate?"

"Maybe so, but I think you're stretching it." Hannah picked up a piece of toast, then put it back down on her plate. "I don't know, Quinn…. This seems awfully far-fetched to me."

He reached across the table and touched her arm. She looked up at him. "Baker visited me quite a bit while I was in the hospital. I got to know him a little better and one day I asked him why he bothered to come see me. He told me had a brother named Chip who was on the bomb squad in Boston. Long story short, the brother got careless during an operation and blew himself up.''

Hannah shook her head. ''I didn't know that, but what has that got to do with—''

Quinn interrupted her. ''I checked out his story, Hannah. Boston Bomb said they'd never had anyone by that name on their team.''

CHAPTER NINE

HER WORDS CAME OUT haltingly. "There could be a million explanations for that, Quinn. Maybe they didn't check well enough or maybe the records are screwed up—"

Quinn's jaw twitched, but his voice stayed calm. "And maybe he was lying."

"Why would he do that?"

"I explained that already."

"For God's sake, Quinn! Do you really think I'm that shallow? I wouldn't fall into Baker's arms just because he helped me with a case."

"This isn't just any case, Hannah. He knows it and so do you. He could have planted that twisted wire you told me about because he would know exactly how much that would bug you."

"You're right," she conceded, "but discovering that wire and linking it back to Mark—that's a huge leap, Quinn. I'm not sure I can jump that high."

"That's because you're thinking like a woman."

She opened her mouth to protest, but he held up his hand. "He wants you. How can he get you? By getting your attention.'' Quinn paused. ''I know how guys like him operate. He would try to impress you, and the best way to do that would be by helping you with the one case he knows you want to solve more than anything....''

Hannah played with the knife beside her now-cold eggs. She'd had similar thoughts herself last night, hadn't she? That Mark wanted to ''help'' her out of her clothes? This took it a little further, though, and she wasn't convinced, but she did know one thing that *was* sure—Quinn understood people. He grasped their motivations and behaviors better than anyone she'd ever known.

She raised her eyes to his. If Quinn thought Mark was involved in this, the chances were damn good Quinn was right.

She'd be a fool to ignore what he was saying.

HANNAH ALLOWED Quinn to go with her to see Inlandson, but not without an argument.

''I've interviewed hundreds of suspects,'' she said as they climbed into her rental car. ''I don't know why you think I can't handle this one.''

''That's not what I think,'' Quinn answered. ''I'm sure you could get everything you need from this guy, but why do it alone if you don't have to? I'm here. Let me help.''

She put the car in Reverse and backed out of her

parking spot, sending him a quick glance. "I'm not comfortable about keeping this from Bobby."

"Nobody's keeping anything from anyone. He's on vacation, Hannah. Do you really think he wants to get a call from D.C. about something this petty? He knew I wanted to come back eventually."

"But this is a temporary situation," she warned. "You don't have a full release."

He rubbed his leg and grimaced. "I'm well aware of that fact. You don't have to remind me."

They left the highway and crossed the bridge before she spoke again. "I have a notebook in my briefcase. Would you get it out and check something for me?"

He retrieved the small leather pad and opened it up.

"Look on the last page," she said. "Lena gave me the name of this place. I wrote it down so I wouldn't forget it. Could you check my notes?"

Just as he said "Golden Light," she slowed the car and whistled. "Never mind. I think I remember now...."

Quinn looked up. A hundred feet ahead, on the right side of the road, a huge complex sprawled behind an eight-foot-tall fence made of wire and topped with a slanted barrier. It enclosed at least ten acres of the low-lying piney woods. Inside the compound, there were a dozen or so large buildings, and one very tall radio tower. The only thing outside the protected area was the neon sign, glowing garishly even though it was barely past ten in the morning.

"Golden Light Ministries," Quinn read. "We Love You, No Matter What. There's a catchy slogan if I ever saw one."

Turning into the shell drive, Hannah rolled down her window and stopped beside a speaker resting on a metal pole. The box crackled to life as Hannah reached out to punch the call button on the digital pad beneath it. Quinn ducked his head and looked through the windshield. Just as he'd expected, a camera sat atop the fence and it was pointed directly at them. He wagged his fingers at the lens as Hannah introduced herself.

"My name is Hannah Crosby, and I'm with the federal government. We're here to see Bob Inlandson, please. He's expecting us."

The gate rolled back silently and Hannah drove through.

"You called ahead?" Quinn glanced across the seat.

"No. Lena did. She said if we just showed up, they'd never let us in. She 'persuaded' them to accept our visit, but don't ask me how."

They followed the signs to the main building and parked. A few moments later, they were walking into an elaborate lobby. Quinn tried not to stare, but it was hard to keep his eyes in line. What wasn't covered in marble was covered with gold. A young man, wearing a suit, sat in the middle of it all behind a tall circular desk. He could have been an executive assistant, except for the look in his eyes. It was coldly assessing.

"I'm Hannah Crosby and this is—"

"He can't go with you," the man said. "Brother Bob specified one person—a woman—could come in and that was it."

Quinn reached for his badge before he remembered he didn't have it. Hannah covered for him smoothly. "This is my associate, Quinn McNichol. He works with me. I'm sure Brother Bob—"

The man started shaking his head before Hannah could finish. "No," he said without hesitation. "I can't let you in. Brother Bob said one and that means one."

Stepping closer to the man's desk, Quinn spotted another camera on the wall behind him. Almost instantly, a door to his right slid open. A stocky man stood on the threshold and Quinn knew they'd found Brother Bob. With a brush cut and a steely gaze, he looked exactly like what he was—an ex-Navy man.

"It's all right, Calvin." He nodded toward Quinn and Hannah. "I promised my cooperation and my promise is my word. I'll talk to them both."

The man clearly wanted to protest, but he nodded.

Hannah and Quinn walked quickly past him to the older man.

Hannah stuck out her hand. "I'm Hannah Crosby. I'm with—"

"I know who you are, ma'am." He didn't take her hand, and she dropped it back to her side in an awkward movement. Turning to Quinn, he said, "You're the one I don't know. Who are you?"

"I work with Hannah." Quinn's voice was measured and deep, and it said in no uncertain terms that he was staying. The preacher's lips thinned, but he had the good sense not to challenge Quinn. Without another word, he went back through the open door.

Hannah looked at Quinn and he shrugged, then they followed the minister into his office.

The room was the direct opposite of the reception area outside. A small metal desk and battered leather chair took up one end, a round table and four chairs were at the other. He waved his hand toward the table. "Have a seat."

Quinn and Hannah went to the table and pulled out chairs. As Quinn sat down, he glanced through the window. The signal tower was directly behind them. It had to be more than three hundred feet high, Quinn estimated. Brother Bob had a helluva range for his radio broadcasts.

Hannah spoke Quinn's thoughts but in nicer

terms. "You have quite a setup here, Mr. Inlandson," she said, tilting her head toward the outer buildings.

"Call me Brother Bob."

She nodded pleasantly, but Quinn knew that was as far as *that* would go. Hannah was a pro; she'd maintain her distance.

"Tell us about your ministry. What exactly do you do from here—"

"You don't want to know about my ministry." He leaned against the windowsill and crossed his arms. "You want to know if I bombed that day-care center over in Destin."

Hannah kept her expression even, but her eyes narrowed. "You're absolutely right," she said after a moment. "So…did you?"

"No, ma'am, I did not. I do not believe in violence as a way to lead people to their righteous choice."

"But you also don't believe in working women, do you?"

"No, ma'am, I don't. I think our community is best served by women who stay home and raise the family and let the men take care of everything else."

"That's not exactly how it's done these days."

"I know that. And so does the Devil."

Quinn watched the exchange with a prejudiced eye. He wasn't much for preachers, but this one was different from what Quinn had expected. For starters, he was a straight talker, stating his case without equivocation.

"Why the security, brother?" Quinn nodded his head toward the fence beyond the window. "Looks like you're expecting an invasion out there."

"I am." The man turned his eyes on Quinn, his gaze intense. Normally Quinn would have felt uneasy under such scrutiny, but he sensed the honesty beneath the fervor. "The world is a troubled place and a fight is coming soon."

"A fight? I thought you didn't believe in violence," Hannah said.

He sent the same kind of look toward Hannah. "I don't. That's why I have the fence. The faithful will be protected."

He dropped his gaze to her left hand. "Are you married, sister?"

His unexpected question clearly threw her off. "No...no, I'm not."

"You should be."

"And why is that?"

"You won't be happy until you are. You won't get your heart's desire and you'll never be content."

Hannah bristled, but Quinn could tell only because he knew her so well. "My heart's desire is not germane to this conversation, Mr. Inlandson. I suggest we stay on the subject."

He shrugged and didn't reply.

Quinn broke the edgy silence that followed. "Tell us where you were two weeks ago when the bombing took place."

He'd been working, Inlandson explained, and was in his office all night. He had the time sheets from their electronic surveillance cameras and could prove when he'd gone inside his office and when he'd come out. He'd be happy to provide them. He'd also had several meetings during those hours. Others could vouch for him.

"You slept here that night?" Hannah asked skeptically.

"I sleep here every night. I live here," he said, pointing to a door Quinn hadn't seen until that point. "My bedroom is through there."

"Where's *your* family?"

He held Hannah's gaze. "My wife is dead, Miss Crosby. She got behind the wheel of our car one night and drove herself and our four children into the Gulf of Mexico. I live alone now."

Quinn's shock registered silently while Hannah's face actually paled. "I'm sorry," she said. "I had no idea...."

"You couldn't have known," he said stoically. "It happened many years ago when we lived somewhere else. She was under a great deal of stress and it caught up with her." He glanced out the window, but Quinn had the feeling he wasn't seeing his sprawling compound; he was seeing five lost faces. He turned back to them. "It was my fault," he said simply. "I didn't make enough money in the military to support a family, and she had to work so we could eat. Taking care of everything got to her."

Quinn continued the questioning after that, but there wasn't a whole lot more to ask the man. He gave them his military history, complete and unabridged. He definitely would know how to build a bomb, but it was just as obvious he'd had nothing to do with any of the crimes. Querying him about his locations during the other bombings, Quinn learned Inlandson had an alibi for almost every date. They left a short time later. A rattled-looking Hannah gave Quinn the keys as they stepped outside.

"You drive" was all she said.

He took them back over the bridge, but when he hit 98, he turned left instead of right. Hannah didn't seem to notice. Staring out the window, she said even less than she had on the way over. Quinn found the road and headed east. To their left, a beach stretched endlessly, the dunes so white they looked like snow, the water green and clear. After a while, he found an empty stretch and a well-tended parking area with a walkover. He parked the car and turned to Hannah.

The fact that they were no longer moving seemed

to surprise her. She glanced around, then looked at him. "What are you doing? We have to get back—"

"What's the hurry?"

"I'm working, in case you've forgotten," she snapped. "I'd like to make my report and figure out what in the hell I'm going to do next."

She was angry and upset. But at the situation, not him.

"I'll tell you what we're going to do next," he said, opening the car door. "We're going for a walk."

He crossed over the dunes and took off his shoes while he waited for her. He heard the car door slam, and a few minutes later she joined him at the bottom of the wooden stairs. "We don't have time for this," she protested. "I need—"

He raised his hand. "You *need* to get some perspective," he interrupted. "Because you're never going to solve this case without it."

Their gazes met, then her shoulders slumped. Brother Bob hadn't been the break she'd wanted.

"It's not the end of the world," Quinn said softly. "C'mon…let's go."

With a lingering reluctance, she slipped out of her shoes and stepped onto the sand. It was cool and smooth beneath her feet, a nice accompaniment to the sound of the waves. They walked in silence, Quinn letting Hannah come to terms on her own with her disappointment. It was the best way for her to handle things, and he knew that from experience. They had been walking for almost fifteen minutes before she spoke.

"I should have let you talk to him," she said. "I really screwed that up."

The intensity in her voice didn't surprise him. Hannah's job meant as much to her as it ever had, maybe even more. He tried to reassure her. "It wouldn't have mattered. And I couldn't have done any better."

"Oh, yes you would have." Her troubled blue eyes met his. "I don't do well with people and I never have. I should stay in the lab."

"Why are you beating yourself up? You asked the right questions and he answered them. What more do you want?"

"I let him get to me." She looked down at her feet and shook her head. "I shouldn't have."

Quinn stopped their progress, his hand on Hannah's arm. It was hard to concentrate on the conversation instead of how her skin felt beneath his touch. In another time, they would have found a secluded spot on the dunes and… He forced himself to focus. "No one knew that but you and me. You're only human, Hannah. You do have feelings. Inlandson zeroed in on them and you reacted. Anyone else would have done the same."

"You wouldn't have." She stared out at the water. "I pressed him because he annoyed me. A good investigator doesn't let emotions get the upper hand like that. Emotions don't have a place in our profession. They aren't productive."

A seagull called out and she turned toward the bird. Still holding her arm, looking at her perfect profile, Quinn realized once more that Hannah wasn't the woman she'd been eight months before. At some point during that time, she'd decided feelings were something to be avoided, emotions useless reactions. The thought distressed him. Had his insistence on doing things his way done this to her?

He didn't really want to know the answer to that question, so instead he tugged her into his arms and began to kiss her.

HIS LIPS TASTED SALTY from the sea air.

Hannah pressed herself to Quinn, her body welcoming the diversion of his kiss. She didn't want to think about the preacher. He'd rattled her way too much when he'd asked her if she was married. Unprepared, she'd been even more shocked by his pronouncement about that state of singleness.

"You won't get your heart's desire and you'll never be content."

She'd felt as if the guy had opened up her chest, reached inside and squeezed her heart dry.

Quinn ran his hands over her shoulders and down her back, bringing her closer. Wrapping her arms around his neck, Hannah made it easy for him. She tilted her head and deepened the kiss. She wanted to pretend they were back on the bayou in his cabin, in his bed. Those few hours had been the best she'd had since Quinn had left. She chastised herself for letting the episode happen, but at the same time, she found herself wishing for a repeat.

Quinn made her feel so special and wanted and…yes…almost content. Almost, but not quite. The awareness of their differences was always there, hovering in the back of her mind. Her desire for children was the obvious difference, but Hannah was beginning to think it wasn't the only one. She had a certain hope in the future—for the future. Did Quinn have that same philosophy? She wasn't sure.

He cradled her head with his hand, his lips leaving hers to gently brush against her throat. For longer than she should have, Hannah let him continue, her arms still around him, her heart beating like crazy. She was sure he could hear it—even the sound of the waves couldn't cover up that kind of erratic pounding. Her body began to do things it shouldn't, and Hannah knew she had to stop herself before she reached a point where that was impossible. Forcing herself to think more and feel less, she was relieved when her good sense finally took over.

She dropped her hands to his chest and gently pushed him back. It took another few moments before he finally lifted his eyes to hers. The desire in their dark depths mirrored her own, but that's all that was there, she told herself. Just desire.

"Why are you stopping us?" he asked. "We're two adults. No commitments to anyone else. We can do what we want…."

He was mocking her words when she'd left last time.

"That's true," she said stiffly, "but—"

He lifted his hand and cupped her jaw. He kissed her again, paused, then kissed her once more. She wasn't sure she'd be able to stand it if he continued much longer.

She pushed him again and this time he stopped. "There's more to a relationship than good sex, Quinn."

"Yeah, but it's a helluva place to start."

"There's more and I want it," she said. "I want a family, a home, a white picket fence. You've never had a desire for any of that."

"*Never* is a pretty definite word to describe what someone else is thinking. Are you sure you know me that well?"

She didn't want to get angry and emotional, but his question triggered all the old feelings. "After everything we've gone through, yes. I *do* believe I know you that well. And if I'm wrong, I think you've had plenty of opportunities to correct me and you haven't.''

The look in his eyes made her heart suddenly stutter. For a single second, she thought he was going to say something that would surprise her. But he didn't.

Instead, they walked back to the car in silence, a renewed tension between them.

QUINN UNLOCKED THE DOOR to his hotel room and stepped inside. Hannah had dropped him off, then left to find the SWAT commander to tell her about the interview. He was grateful to have the time to himself. Going with her this morning, being so close to her and wanting her so much, had been tough, especially knowing as he did that they still didn't want the same things. She continued to want a family and he continued—more than ever—to think that unwise.

As if that wasn't bad enough, he hadn't anticipated the extra stress of watching her work.

He should be back at work, dammit. He told himself he was more than capable and that every day he was getting stronger. The temporary status *would* turn permanent. Everything would be fine. He continued in that vein for a few more minutes, then he limped to the mirror, looked at himself and cursed again.

Like hell it would....

Quinn could do a lot of things, but lie wasn't one of them. Not even to himself.

His leg had been hurting like bloody hell and a dull ache had lodged itself inside his chest. Ever since he'd gotten to Florida, he'd felt tired. He wasn't completely well...and he was beginning to wonder if he would ever feel good again.

How could he expect Hannah to want him if he couldn't even hold down a job? Everything he believed in and stood for—responsibility, accountability, independence—rested on being able to take care of himself and others. He wasn't the kind of man who could sit at a desk all day and a disability check wasn't an option. Even if they were to miraculously come to an agreement on the family issue, he didn't want children he couldn't afford to raise.

What was he going to do if he couldn't go back to EXIT?

SITTING IN A CHAIR across from Lena's desk, Hannah summarized the interview with Bob Inlandson. Her mind wasn't really on the debriefing, though. It was back with Quinn on the beach, his arms embracing her, his lips covering hers. They were heading for dangerous ground and she had no idea how to stop the slide.

A question from Lena brought Hannah's attention back into the room. "No, no...I'm glad you brought me down here. It looked like a good possibility to me, too," Hannah said. "But he's clear. There's no way Inlandson could have done this bombing or, as far as I can tell, any of the others."

She pulled the time sheets and flyers the preacher had given her from her briefcase and tossed them on Lena's desk. "His alibis are tight, too. He has a computer-based security system and the printouts confirm he was in his office the night of the bombing. They could have been altered, of course, but he had flyers for all the revivals he's held over the past few years and they confirmed the reports. For the most part, the dates put him across the country when the other explosions took place."

Lena shook her head. "I should have known better. This would have been way too easy." She hesitated, then said, "I *want* this bomber, Hannah. We don't like his kind in our neighborhood."

"Nobody wants him more than me, but Brother Bob is not a bomber. He's...not the one."

"You're sure?"

"Absolutely." Hannah took a moment to gather her thoughts. The personal exchange with Inlandson had rattled Hannah. Talking with Quinn had helped settle her down, but her reaction had no place here, either. She had to be as objective as she could with Lena. "I obviously don't agree with his philosophy, but a lot of people must feel the way he does. He has an incredible setup out there and money is not a problem. I was all ready to dislike him, but there's something about the man. He's very open, very up front. Not your usual, run-of-the-mill religious fanatic. I'm convinced he's clear."

"What did Baker think of him?" Lena had met Mark the night he'd come into town. He'd gone directly to her office and introduced himself. Then he'd hit on her. He'd made quite an impression.

"Baker didn't go with me. I sent him back to New Orleans after a quick stop in Pensacola."

"You went by yourself?"

"Not exactly."

Lena raised an eyebrow and waited for more.

"Quinn McNichol went with me," Hannah said. "Quinn's the tech who was injured during the New Orleans blast. He showed up unexpectedly with a temporary release from his medical leave so I let him come. He's very good with people."

Lena's look was sharp; she heard the underlying emotion in Hannah's voice. But she was smart enough not to ask about it and Hannah let the explanation stop there. They discussed the case for a bit longer, then Bradley Thompson appeared in the doorway.

"Sorry to interrupt," he said. "But we got a problem."

"You're not interrupting," Lena said. "And if you were, that'd be okay. What's going on?"

"You know that warrant DPD was supposed to serve on that guy east of town?"

Lena narrowed her eyes. "The meth guy?"

"That's him. They caught him outside and served the warrant, but now they're worried about going in. He's acting a little too weird."

"Not good."

Bradley nodded. "My sentiments, exactly."

"NOPD sees a lot of labs," Hannah said. "They're nasty."

"Until now, we haven't handled that many," Lena answered. "A few mobile ones have come through—some guys using the old family Winnebago—but nothing like this. Apparently this guy's really set up shop."

The clandestine drug labs used deadly chemicals to make methamphetamine, and the risks to the investigating officers were incredible. If the chemicals didn't get you, then the booby traps would. The men running the manufacturing process didn't take their security lightly.

"Maybe we can help," Hannah suggested. "You want me and Quinn to tag along?"

Lena looked as if Hannah had just offered her a million bucks. "Oh, man, would you?"

"Sure." Hannah stood. "We'd be happy to do what we can."

Lena jumped up from behind her desk and grabbed her SWAT team jacket. Tossing it to Hannah, she grinned. "Then congratulations. You're now a member of the Emerald Coast SWAT team. Let's grab your fellow and head out."

CHAPTER TEN

HANNAH HAD CALLED AHEAD and Quinn was waiting for them outside.

"Omigod..." Lena sent Hannah a quick glance as she wheeled the Suburban into the hotel's parking lot. "You didn't tell me the guy looked like that. I would have driven faster if I'd known I was picking up *him*."

Hannah couldn't help but laugh. Quinn had traded the jacket and slacks he'd worn to Inlandson's for jeans and a black T-shirt. A *tight* black T-shirt that emphasized his now-chiseled body and hardened face. With his wind-ruffled hair and stubbly jaw, he *was* handsome. Dangerously handsome.

"He *is* gorgeous...." she said softly, almost to herself.

"But?" Lena headed the truck to the curb where he waited.

"But what?" Hannah looked across the seat.

"You tell me. I thought for sure I heard a 'but' in there somewhere." Lena raised an eyebrow, then threw the truck into Park. "There usually is one with a guy who looks like that."

Saving Hannah an answer, Quinn opened the back door and climbed inside, extending his hand over the seat to Lena and introducing himself. With a conspiratorial grin in Hannah's direction, Lena shook Quinn's hand. "Nice to meet you, Officer McNichol."

"Call me Quinn."

She nodded and put the truck in gear, shooting out of the parking lot. "I'm Lena."

She launched into an explanation of what they were doing. Hannah could feel Quinn's stare on the back of her neck. He missed nothing—later she'd have to face his questions about that smile.

"We think it's a Nazi lab," Lena was saying. "Not a good thing."

"I've heard about those, but we haven't encountered any yet." Leaning forward, Quinn sat with his hands over the front seat. "Tell me more."

"Well, they call them Nazi labs because they use a different method to make the meth—with a recipe out of Nazi Germany." She looked in her side mirror and switched lanes quickly. "It requires anhydrous ammonia, which makes things easier and faster. A good cooker can make a batch in half the time. Plus it's very portable."

"Anhydrous ammonia? That's wicked stuff."

Lena nodded in Hannah's direction. "One good whiff and your lungs are jelly. To make things even more fun, if the metals they use—sodium and lithium—ignite, then we're in major trouble. Water can't put out the flames. They burn even hotter if they come in contact with it." She gunned the vehicle around a slow-moving truck. "You guys know how explosive this crap is. All it takes is a wrong look and it goes up. The mess is even worse then. EPA has to get involved in the cleanup and the cost is outrageous, not to mention the hazards."

They continued the discussion, Lena driving fast but carefully. Twenty minutes later, she made a quick turn off the main highway and two minutes after that they were deep in the woods. The tall trees looming on either side of the road made Hannah think of a green tunnel. The feeling wasn't pleasant and neither was the smell that filled the cab of the SUV. She couldn't hold back a gag.

Lena gave her a sympathetic look. "It's bad, isn't it? They use a lot of ammonia."

Quinn immediately put his hand on her shoulder. "You okay?"

Hannah nodded, then caught Lena's curious look. Now there would be even more explaining to do.

They pulled up to a collection of vehicles, including the SWAT RV, a large Haz-Mat truck and three black-and-whites. Lena led them to the RV, and it was only after they stepped inside that Hannah saw the lab itself. Parked directly in front of them, it was housed in an old, beat-up camper. As Lena introduced Quinn to everyone, Hannah stared at it through the windshield.

The once-smooth aluminum shell was pock-marked and grimy, a thick layer of leaves, dirt and netting camouflaging its sides and top. Six rusting propane tanks were propped against one end, and a collection of overflowing trash containers decorated the other. The screen door dangled from a single hinge at the top.

Hannah turned as Lena's voice rose. "What do you mean he won't tell you?"

Beck Winters filled the center aisle of the RV. The negotiator shrugged his huge shoulders. "The guy's not talking, Lena. The uniforms caught him before he made it inside and they served the warrant, but all he did was smile and invite them to search the place. Something's up, but right now he's not saying what."

Quinn spoke quietly. "He doesn't have to explain."

Lena's voice was curt as she switched her attention to Quinn. "You think the place is booby-trapped?"

"Of course it is." Quinn tilted his head. "But

don't take my word for it. Look for yourself and tell me what you think.''

In unison, everyone turned and stared.

After a moment, the commander turned back. ''I see a shit hole that might catch on fire at any moment…but I have a feeling you see something different.''

Quinn pointed. ''He's got a new doormat.''

Lena glanced back and so did Hannah. A heavy hemp doormat covered the area just in front of the trailer's door. It was completely free of dirt, the large Welcome on it easy to read even from their distant spot. Hannah understood instantly.

But Lena frowned. ''He does, doesn't he? That's weird.''

Quinn lifted a nearby pair of binoculars to his eyes. ''The tag's still on it. Your man shops at Target. That's probably where he got the wire, too.'' He lowered the glasses and looked at them. ''The one that's leading to the pressure device underneath his brand-new mat.''

Shaking her head, Lena soundly cursed the cooker…and then his mother.

Quinn seconded her opinion.

THE STATE BOYS WERE the closest bomb team. Lena called and explained the situation, then requested backup. The lieutenant who answered said they'd assist but no one could come out until the following day. It wasn't an emergency, anyway, he drawled, and since the big guys were there already, why didn't she just use them? Save the state the trouble and some money. Lena frowned and hung up, turning to Hannah and Quinn. "I shouldn't have told 'em you were here."

Quinn looked at Hannah and she confirmed his unspoken question. "Doesn't matter to us." He shrugged. "We'd rather be doing something than sitting around and watching, anyway."

Lena grinned and then they went to work.

Rigging some homemade equipment from what the SWAT team had available, Hannah and Quinn cleared the area, then studied the device under the doormat. The possibility existed that it was only a dummy—they sometimes were—but Quinn took no chances. An anxious half hour followed as they decided what to do. Finally Quinn began delicately scooping out the dirt from beneath the device.

Ten minutes later, they were finished…and so was the device. Hannah exhaled.

After that, they entered the trailer and quickly located three other devices, armed and ready to explode, two pipe bombs with fuses and one half-finished mollie. The Molotov was stable, unless there had been a fire, but the pipe bombs were another story. Any hapless officer searching the camper could have been injured severely, if not killed. Exhausted but pumped, they didn't finish until well after dark.

Lena shook their hands and thanked them profusely. "I can't believe what you guys found. My God, this could have been such a disaster...."

"We were happy to help." Wiping his face on the sleeve of his T-shirt, Quinn stood on the "sidewalk" they'd made from crime-scene tape. Outside the area was no man's land—mines were a definite possibility, they'd explained. "Just another day at the office. Right, Hannah?"

Smiling at Lena, Quinn glanced over at Hannah, his eyes flashing. She tried to avoid their draw but gave up, admitting to herself how impossible that was. Being here with Quinn had made Hannah remember just how great they were together. His strengths complemented her weaknesses and vice versa. No challenge seemed too big to overcome, and even though her heart had pounded when he'd stepped over that mat, she trusted Quinn explicitly. He knew how to do his job and he knew how to do it well.

They said goodbye to everyone at the scene, then one of the officers gave them a ride back to their hotel. As the young woman in black drove off into the darkness and Hannah unlocked her door, Quinn suggested a late dinner. Hannah wasn't surprised;

it's how they'd always decompressed after completing an anxiety-filled job.

And after dinner, they'd always made love.

Her fingers on the doorknob, she hesitated.

"It's only a meal, Hannah." He held out his hands. They were streaked with dirt and grime just as her own were. "No strings."

They both knew he was lying, of course. There were always strings where she and Quinn were concerned.

But he didn't wait for her to say yes. Heading for his own room, he spoke over his shoulder without looking back. "I'll see you in twenty minutes."

She unlocked the door and stepped inside her dim hotel room, the sudden quiet an unwelcome accompaniment to her swirling thoughts. Where were they going? What were they doing? Quinn clearly didn't want any more of a commitment than he had before, but the connection between them was as strong as ever. Was it up to her? Was he waiting for her to walk away again? She leaned against the door and closed her eyes, an unexpected weakness sweeping over her. She wasn't sure she could withstand that kind of pain again.

But then…

Maybe she was demanding too much. Maybe the ideal life she longed for simply didn't exist anymore. People lived together all the time without marriage, without bonds. They even had families without the benefit of a legal arrangement. Why did she have to have it all? Quinn clearly loved her. And dammit to hell, she loved him, too. Wasn't that enough?

She opened her eyes and stumbled into the bathroom, her questions following her under the steaming showerhead. She let the water pound her until a loud knocking brought her out of her reverie.

Dripping wet, she grabbed her robe, threw it on and ran toward the door. When she swung it open, a waiter stood on the doorstep, a laden room-service cart before him.

He smiled uncertainly. "You ordered dinner?"

"Yes, she did." Quinn came up to the man and handed him a wad of bills. "I'll take it from here."

Hannah stepped back as Quinn rolled in the cart. "You said twenty minutes," she protested. "It's only been—"

"Thirty," he said. "Look."

She glanced at the clock beside the bed. He was right. She'd stood in the shower half an hour, her jumbled-up thoughts preoccupying her as completely as they had back at the bayou. Which immediately made her remember what had followed *that* shower.

Locking her gaze with Quinn's, Hannah began to shake her head. Dinner in her room while wearing

a bathrobe was not what she'd had in mind. "I—
I'd rather dress," she said, clutching her lapels.
"Don't you want to go downstairs and—"

"I'm tired and so are you. Let's not make this a
bigger deal than it has to be."

Taken aback by his words, she looked at him a
little closer. They'd worked hard for hours and she'd
never even given a second thought about his stam-
ina. Did he look more weary than usual? She
couldn't tell, but she also knew Quinn would die
before he'd let her know he wasn't at his best.

"You're absolutely right," she said.

His gaze was noncommittal. "Dry off, then come
back and sit down. I'd like to eat before it gets
cold."

She did as he suggested. By the time they finished
the steaks and salads he'd ordered, Hannah had finally relaxed. Chuckling over something Quinn said
about the trailer they'd searched, she thought about
how long it'd been since she'd done that very thing.
Laughter—as well as love—had been missing from
her life for months.

Her realization must have shown on her face. A
moment later Quinn leaned across the table and
picked up her hand. She didn't resist because she
couldn't—whenever he touched her, her brain short-
circuited.

"I love it when you laugh like that." His thumb

caressed the inside of her palm, sending shivers up her arm and straight into her heart. "You should do it more often."

"You're right about that." Her agreement obviously surprised him. "I guess nothing has seemed amusing to me lately. I've gotten a little too intense."

"Why is that?" His eyes searched her face. "You didn't let that pipe bomb thing get to you, did you?"

It took a second for her to understand. "You mean the incident with the Andros? When you were in the hospital?"

He nodded.

She shook her head slowly. "Not really. That only happened because I was tired. It was stupid, of course, and I was horrified, but no one was ever in real danger. I had the Andros pointed away. Even if it'd gone off, we would have been okay."

He seemed lost in thought for a moment, then he asked, "If that's not what changed you, then what was it? You guard yourself more closely, watch what you do and say. Why is that? What happened to the open, up-front woman I used to know?" He hesitated, his expression pained. "Was it…us?"

Hannah pulled her fingers from his grip and stood. There was a small patio off her room that looked out toward the Gulf. Walking to it, she opened the sliding glass door and paused in the doorway to think about her answer, the breeze billowing the draperies on either side of her. After a bit, she crossed her arms and spoke, surprised at her own candor. "That woman decided it was time to be more careful with her emotions."

He rose and followed her to the doorway, pausing at her side. His aftershave mingled with the fresh salt air, and without any warning, Hannah felt as if she were dangling over a precipice a hundred feet up. When he reached out and caressed her throat with the back of one finger, she fell...all the way down.

"I liked the old one better," he said softly. "She wasn't afraid of anything."

"Well, she should have been." Hannah tried to steel herself against his touch. "There are too many ways to get hurt out there. You have to protect yourself if you want to survive."

"But is surviving the same as living?"

Her heart thrummed painfully against her ribs. "Probably not...but sometimes surviving is all you *can* do."

His fingers had made their way to the base of her throat. As she spoke, he spread them above her breasts and she felt as if he'd touched her with a torch.

"I know all about surviving," he said simply. "I do it every day."

QUINN WILLED HER TO SAY something, to do something, but she seemed to sense his need and resisted. This was something new, as well. She'd become more adept at reading people.

"Tell me what you're thinking," he demanded, his chest going tight.

"I think we're talking about two different things," she said carefully. "I'm talking about my heart and you're talking about your health."

Quinn recognized a challenge when he heard one. If he wanted a future with her, this was the perfect time to tell her.

But what could he say?

This afternoon, they'd worked so closely he'd felt as if they had one body, one heart, one mind. Only once had she seemed to hesitate and that was when he'd first stepped over the mat and entered the trailer. But his own heart had been racing at that point, too. Anyone with half a brain would have been scared. The incident proved one thing to him, however, one very important thing. He and Hannah *could* work together just fine. If Bobby still believed that was a problem, he didn't know what he was talking about.

None of that really mattered, though, if Quinn didn't get a medical release. Even if they could come to some agreement, the dream Hannah had of a family would never come true. Having children and not being able to support them was just as bad as not being there at all.

He looked into Hannah's bright blue eyes, his heart beating so fast it felt as if it might burst out of his chest. He had no idea what to say, but he started to talk, anyway, knowing all his reactions and feelings about the accident had somehow gotten tangled up and mixed together with their relationship. As clever as he was supposed to be with people, however, Quinn had no idea how to unknot the mess.

"I'm talking about the same thing you are, Hannah. My life has been hell for the past nine months. I've felt like a ghost, and half the time I wished I was. If I'd died in that explosion, neither of us would have gone through the pain we have."

"Don't say that," she said with a horrified look. "If you'd died…" She couldn't finish the sentence.

"You're the only reason I didn't, Hannah. You kept me going, sitting there day after day…even when you didn't want to. Why did you hang in there with me? Why did you give me so much of yourself when I was in the hospital…and then leave?"

"I loved you." Her breath was soft against his face and he realized that she'd moved closer to him and his arms were around her. "That's what people do for the ones they love."

"But?"

"But I had to take care of myself, too, Quinn. I had to find someone who shared my dreams of a family."

"And did you?"

She waited a long time to answer. "No," she said finally. "I didn't find anyone. But I didn't look, either. And I think we both know why."

Her words reached deep inside him and touched his heart. Pulling her toward him, he kissed her. Her lips melted under his and she opened herself to him, her tongue seeking his, her hands slipping under his shirt to search for the heat of his body. In a matter of minutes, their clothes were off and they'd stumbled to the bed on the other side of the room.

WHEN HANNAH WOKE UP the next morning, Quinn was behind her, cradling her body into the curve of his own, one hand on the rise of her hip and the other draped over her shoulder.

She'd never felt so loved.

Hannah eased from beneath Quinn's embrace and stood. She could barely resist the urge to reach out and smooth his hair, but she didn't want to wake him—she'd rather fill her eyes with the sight of his lean form in the sheets. Beneath the hard exterior was a man unlike any she'd ever known. No one else could even come close to making her feel the way Quinn did. Was she prepared to sacrifice that just because she wanted more?

She padded to the sliding glass window and looked out at the rising sun as if it could help her decide. The light spreading over the water was golden, streaks of peach and lavender leading her eyes into the clouds. The answer she sought wasn't there, though—it was buried somewhere in her soul, and if she truly wanted the truth, then she had some thinking to do.

The sudden shattering ring of the telephone sent her thoughts flying. Pivoting, she dashed toward the bed, but Quinn had already reached out and answered it. Propping himself up on one elbow, he listened intently for a moment, then said, ''I'll tell her right now. We can be there in ten minutes.'' He started to hang up, but stopped, the caller obviously saying something more.

Wearing a puzzled frown, Hannah came to the edge of the bed as Quinn continued to listen. He held up his hand as if to stop her, then spoke. ''I understand,'' he said, nodding his head. ''That's not a problem, believe me. She'll be there as soon as she can.''

He hung up the phone, then met Hannah's stare. ''You aren't going to believe this,'' he said.

Hannah's every nerve jumped to attention. She dropped to the edge of the bed. ''What is it?''

"That was Lena. She said a state trooper just called her. He's arrested a guy who claims to be Mr. Rogers. He's in a jail in Tallahassee and he wants to talk to you."

CHAPTER ELEVEN

HANNAH'S LOOK OF PURE shock morphed into disbelief. "Me? He wants to talk to me?"

"That's what Lena said."

"Why was he arrested? Is she sure it's him? Why does he want to see me?" Shooting questions over her shoulder, Hannah jumped up and ran to her suitcase where she grabbed a handful of clothes. She went into the bathroom, but the stream of queries kept coming. "Is he in a federal prison or a county jail? Did she call Bobby, too?"

When she paused to catch a breath, Quinn got in some answers. "They stopped the guy for a broken taillight and found RDX in his trunk. He's being held in the county jail right now. And I don't know if she called Bobby or not."

She popped out of the bathroom door. Her blouse hung crooked because she'd buttoned it wrong and her hair was sticking out in five places. She'd never looked so beautiful to him as she did when she asked her next question.

"Can you go with me, Quinn? I don't want to do this alone."

He got out of bed and came to where she stood. "I can't go with you, Hannah."

"But I need you! You're so much better than me at this kind of thing—"

"The guy told Lena he wouldn't talk to anyone but you. You could lose him completely if I went with you."

Clutching his arm, Hannah spoke in a worried voice. "But I'm not sure I can do this. I didn't do such a great job with Bob Inlandson—"

"You did fine with Brother Bob." He put his hands on her shoulders and squeezed them lightly. "And you'll do the same here. You're as good an interrogator as anyone I know. And you've got an incredible advantage."

She looked at him doubtfully. "Oh, yeah? What?"

"You're you. Obviously somewhere along the way, he heard something about you and he's interested. He asked for you by name."

"But how? And why?"

"Who knows? Who cares? Use it to your advantage—that's all that counts."

"And exactly how do I do that?"

"Play him, Hannah, play him. Manipulate him

into telling you what you want to know by giving him what he wants.''

''What *does* he want?''

''He wants you, of course.''

''Hey, hey…that's going a little too far—''

''For God's sake, Hannah, I mean psychologically….'' Quinn shook his head. Maybe he'd been a little too quick in his assessment of her growing intuition. She was still as literal as ever. ''Tell him something about yourself. Give him little pieces of information. Make him feel like the two of you are going to be each other's new best friend. Just remember what I told you. He's obsessive and very much into control. Let him feel like he's running the show and you'll get everything you need, I promise you.''

She looked so uncertain he wondered for a second if she *could* handle it. But he wondered for *only* a second. She'd come through for the team, if for no other reason.

He looked into the blueness of her eyes and spoke softly. ''You can do this, Hannah. You can put this guy away, once and for all. You can do it for me…and for the kids who died. They deserve some justice. This is your chance to give it to them.''

QUINN GAVE HANNAH THE other few details he knew as they drove to Lena's office.

"His name is Daniel Pinkley. He claimed he did the Destin job the minute the officer spotted the RDX. He seemed pretty proud of himself."

Hannah gripped the steering wheel so tightly she was afraid the damn thing might snap off. She tried to relax her fingers, but they wouldn't budge. They seemed as determined as her gut to reflect her growing anxiety. Quinn's words of reassurance were great, but she still had her doubts. Her strong suit had never been dealing with people, and now the entire case might rest on just that.

They arrived at the SWAT offices and went directly to Lena's desk. Hannah tried not to show her nervousness as Lena greeted them.

"Have the state guys done a background check on him yet?" Quinn asked.

"I'm sure it's in the works, but I haven't been told," Lena answered.

"Prints wouldn't help us." Hannah spoke without thinking. "We've never gotten a single one from any of the scenes."

"Well, they wouldn't hurt. I can take them with me tonight when I go back to New Orleans," Quinn replied.

Hannah looked at Lena. "How do I get to Tallahassee?"

"You can fly from Fort Walton but that means going through Atlanta. There are no direct flights.

The quickest way is to drive.'' Lena pointed out her office window where the sunlight was beginning to stream in. ''Head east on I-10 and don't stop till you've gone 160 miles. That'll be Tallahassee. I can give you a bubble or loan you a unit—take your pick.''

The offer of a temporary red light would speed the journey, as would one of the big black Suburbans, but the guy wasn't going to go anywhere before she could arrive. Unless he changed his mind and found himself an attorney.

That idea was all it took.

''I'll take the SUV,'' she said. ''*And* the bubble.''

Lena nodded approvingly and stood up from behind her desk. ''There aren't any big towns between here and there, but you gotta watch out for the local cops in Ponce de Leon. They like to stop our guys just to see what's going on. Barring that, you should be able to get there in two and a half hours if you keep your speed under seventy.''

She walked around to where Hannah waited. ''Nail this son of a bitch, Hannah,'' Lena said softly. ''If he's our man, he needs to be put away.''

DURING THE DRIVE TO Tallahassee, Hannah could have tried to sort out everything and develop some kind of plan. She could have concentrated on what had happened between her and Quinn. She could have tried to come to terms with the confusion in her heart and mind.

But she didn't.

Instead, she blanked her mind and watched the passing scenery as if she had nothing more important to do. That's what Quinn had told her to do as he'd kissed her goodbye.

"Don't get too psyched," he'd said. "Take it easy and let him lead the conversation. He obviously has an agenda, so let that develop as naturally as you can."

She'd held on to his arm. "I wish you'd go with me."

"I know." His expression had softened as much as it could. "But this is the best way. You go talk to him and I'll work the prints. And corner Baker. I have some questions for him."

"Is that really necessary now?"

His eyes had hardened at her question. "Absolutely. We don't know if Pinkley is for real or not."

She almost felt sorry for Mark. "What are you going to ask him?"

"I don't know," he'd said. "But it'll come to me. In the meantime, Bobby's back. He cut his vacation short and I want to talk to him." Something else came into his eyes at that point. "I've got to schedule another appointment with Barroso, too."

He'd pulled her into his arms then and kissed her

until she was dizzy. With her head spinning, she'd climbed into the Suburban and driven away.

Before she knew it, Hannah had entered the outskirts of Tallahassee. Glancing down at her notes, she read the address of the Leon County Jail. The facility was located on Appleyard Drive—a name that brought forth a lot of images, none of them a jail. Hannah took the closest exit off I-10 and easily found the huge complex. The staff was courteous and efficient, and after she'd talked briefly with the man in charge of the facility, a uniformed officer took over, escorting her to the proper unit. As they walked, Hannah looked at the paperwork she'd been given.

A photograph of Pinkley clipped to the file showed exactly what she'd expected. A totally nondescript individual. He looked to be in his late thirties or early forties, was balding and slightly overweight. He could have been her mailman or the guy at the video store, or the dentist who lived next door. He was one of those people Hannah thought of as invisible. She shivered as they passed under an air-conditioning vent, but her tremor had nothing to do with the cold blast of air.

The officer didn't notice. He was busy explaining the jail's famous work-crew program. Every inmate worked six days a week, six to ten hours a day. In black-and-white-striped clothing, they picked up trash, cleaned graffiti and generally displayed themselves as a crime-prevention tool.

Hannah made the appropriate sounds of approval, her attention returning to the intake pages.

Pinkley had grown up in Texas, joined the army at eighteen, done his two-year hitch, then attended a junior college near Colorado Springs. He listed his occupation as ''computer consultant,'' but his work history was far from professional. In the past ten years he'd held eleven different positions. He claimed to be married, but no wife's name was given. Hannah wondered what that meant as the guard opened a door and led her into a small room with a desk and two chairs.

''You can wait here,'' he said politely. ''It'll take a few minutes for me to go get him.''

Hannah nodded calmly, but her anxiety was growing with every second. She wanted Quinn. She wanted help. She wanted…out.

But that wasn't an option.

It felt as if a year had passed before the guard returned. Finally, through the window, she caught a glance of him and someone else. The door opened and a man who matched the photograph in her hand shuffled in. He kept his eyes down. His ankles were shackled and he seemed unstable, but every hair was in place. His jail uniform was just as neat, his shirt, buttoned to the collar, tucked into his pants precisely. She'd heard about inmates putting their clothing under their mattresses at night to give them the appearance of being ironed, but Pinkley's looked as if they'd come straight from the dry cleaners.

The guard helped him into the chair opposite Hannah's, then attached his cuffs to rings on the underside of the table. When he finished, the guard nodded toward the door. "I'll be right out there. Let me know when you're finished."

She watched the guard leave, took a deep breath and turned to Pinkley. That's when he lifted his eyes to hers.

Hannah sucked in a breath and held it. She'd never seen such emptiness in anyone's gaze.

QUINN'S TRIP BACK to New Orleans was uneventful, and he hoped his meeting with Bobby would be the same. Even more important, though, he had a question for Bobby about the long-ago pipe bomb incident. When Hannah had talked about it, she'd given the accident a different spin entirely, making it sound much less dangerous than Bobby had. Quinn had no doubt Hannah was telling the truth, but so what had Bobby been doing?

In the meantime, he had Baker to handle.

Back in New Orleans, Quinn headed straight for EXIT's headquarters. Striding into the building, the first person he saw was Jolie.

She grinned hugely, then grabbed him and pulled him into an empty office, her expression going from delighted to anxious in the space of two seconds.

"You lookin' good, baby, good!" she cooed the minute the door closed behind them, "but you better be up to your fightin' strength 'cause that Bobby, he be looking for you, cher, and it ain't to welcome you back, no."

"He's mad?"

"As an ol' wet hen!" Her fingernails dug into his arm. "You need to be careful, Quinnie." Her eyes latched on to his, all signs of her playfulness disappearing. "I don't trust that man, no, and you shouldn't, either."

"What are you saying, Jolie? What do you know that I don't?"

Dropping her hand, she blinked and shook her head. "Jus' watch your back, baby. Thas all. Watch your back."

She gave him a hard hug and a more-than-just-friends kiss, then slipped out of the office. A few seconds later, Quinn followed. Jolie liked to be mysterious, but her warning had a ring of authenticity he couldn't ignore.

Quinn entered the bullpen and was greeted with enthusiasm from all of the techs. They patted him on the back and welcomed him into their midst as if he'd never left. It felt incredibly good and made him even more determined to become a permanent member of the team once again.

Then from the corner of his eye, Quinn saw Mark Baker. The tech leaned against the open doorway to the coffee room and watched from a distance. When the excitement died down, he made his way toward Quinn, his manner so casual it seemed suspicious...at least to Quinn.

"Hey, Baker," Quinn said, sticking out his hand. "I see you made it back from Destin."

The younger man nodded. "As did you. Where's Hannah?"

His question cleared up one issue. Baker obviously had no idea who Hannah was talking to at the moment. If Bobby knew about Pinkley he hadn't mentioned it to the rest of the team.

"She had to stay behind," Quinn said in a noncommittal voice. "Something came up."

"What kind of something?"

Quinn tilted his head toward an empty desk in the corner of the room. It had to be Hannah's—there was a dead fern on one edge and a drooping ivy on the other. Without comment, Baker followed him to the desk and they both sat down.

"So what's she doing?" Baker asked. "Her preacher-man prove to be the devil?"

Quinn shook his head. "Nah, he's clear. She just stayed to take care of some paperwork." The lie came easily. "We helped the SWAT team clean up a meth lab the other day and it seemed easier to do the reports while she was there instead of here."

"Was it a bad one?"

"Coulda been. The cooker was a little too happy about us arriving and that tipped them off. We found a wired pressure-release device and some other little presents he'd left behind. Nothing too complicated." He paused and casually shifted the conversation. "What'd you think of the scene down there, Baker? You think it's Mr. Rogers?"

"I'm not sure," he said. "Looks like it could be, but who knows?"

The ambivalent question was so unlike Baker's usual blustery tirades, it made him more cautious. "*We* gotta know," Quinn answered. "I'm getting sick and tired of this SOB slipping away."

"He's a smooth one, that's for sure." Baker's knuckles were white around his mug, but he sipped his coffee as if he didn't have a care in the world. "Not to change the subject or anything, but you and Hannah… You guys together again?"

Focusing on his next question—which he'd wanted to be about Baker's "brother" on the Boston team—Quinn took a moment too long to reply.

"I guess that answers that, huh?" Baker grinned, but it was rueful. "I knew you'd never be able to stay away from her. If I had a woman like her, I'd feel the same way, that's for sure.''

Abandoning his previous query, Quinn looked at the man across the desk from him. ''What if you had Hannah yourself?''

Quinn's question clearly startled him, but Baker recovered quickly. ''She's never given me a chance, McNichol, and that's the God's honest truth. It's not for lack of trying, either.''

His candidness surprised Quinn. He'd expected some kind of bullshit answer. ''So much for friends, huh?''

Baker grinned again and shrugged. ''Hey, man, what can I say? I love a challenge.'' He stood. ''I'd better get back to my desk, though. We got a hundred pounds of dynamite missing from a contractor in Atlanta who was remodeling the FBI offices, if you can believe that. The guy who owns the company's going to have a stroke if we don't find the crap pretty soon. He thinks his ex-wife might have taken it to rig his Mercedes SL.''

Quinn stood up, too. ''Be a damn shame to destroy a car like that.''

Baker laughed and started back to his side of the bullpen, but when Quinn called his name he turned.

''While I was in Destin, Hannah and I decided it might be a good idea for me to go back through some of the old case files. You know, just to review everything. She said you probably knew where they were since she'd asked you to find the one on the bombing in Mississippi. You got those handy, by any chance?''

Anyone else wouldn't have noticed, but Quinn wasn't anyone else.

Baker stiffened imperceptibly, then swallowed hard—so hard his throat moved up and down. Had Quinn been a little closer, he was sure he could have heard the man gulp. ''Don't tell Hannah, but I took those babies home,'' he said smoothly. ''I'll bring them back tomorrow if that'll work for you.''

Quinn met his eyes with a steady look. ''That would be fine,'' he said. ''I'll look for you tomorrow.''

With a quick nod, Baker turned and went back to his desk, where he sat down and began to study a pile of paper with concentrated effort. Quinn headed to Bobby's office, but before he stepped inside, he sent one last look over his shoulder.

Baker had forgotten all about his paperwork and had been staring at Quinn's back. Seeing Quinn, he dropped his gaze with a guilty start and reached for his report once more.

Quinn wasn't a betting man, but had he been he would have placed money that Mark Baker was hiding something. Something important. Quinn could only wonder if that something might be attempted murder. Of himself.

HANNAH SPOKE FIRST. "Mr. Pinkley, I'm with a federal branch of the government called EXIT. That stands for—"

"The Explosives and Incendiary Team." His voice was as flat as his gaze, with no inflection or accent of any kind. A machine could have been speaking and she couldn't have heard any difference.

"That's correct. And my name is—"

"Hannah Melissa Crosby."

Remembering Quinn's advice, she forced herself to smile and tried to ignore the tightness in her gut. "That's correct, as well. I came here today because I was told you wanted to see me."

"I do, but I've only allotted twenty minutes for you in my schedule." His lips moved minutely in what she assumed he meant to be a smile. "I believe that will be sufficient, though. Do you know why I wanted to see you?"

"No, I'm afraid not. Why don't you tell me?"

"You're a bomb tech," he said. "One of the best. I've read about you. I saw the article and the photograph in that newsletter. You know? The one the kids get?"

Hannah needed a moment, then she remembered.

A few years back, she'd done an interview for a children's weekly newspaper, explaining what the team did and how they worked. They'd published a snapshot of her standing beside the TVC rig. Cold fingers traced her backbone at the idea of this man holding that paper and looking at her picture.

"You must have children, then," she said politely. "Did they bring you the paper to read?"

"I don't have children." Again the lift of his lips. "I found the newspaper...somewhere."

She nodded, then waited. And waited some more. Finally he spoke again.

"You're an expert."

"I do my job," she answered, "the best way I can. I don't know if that makes me an expert or not, but that's what I do."

"I do that, too. I'm an expert."

"That's nice." Hannah licked her dry lips. "What exactly are you an expert in, Mr. Pinkley?"

"I build bombs."

Hannah froze. She hadn't expected it to be this easy.

A tinge of pride slipped into the mechanical voice before he could stop it, his words as precise as his appearance. "I'm very good at what I do."

She was trying to decide how to reply when he suddenly leaned forward. Restrained by his shackles

he couldn't get too close, but Hannah flinched in-
stinctively. He didn't seem to notice.

"Do you live alone?" He blinked, his eyelids
dropping over his empty gaze like a shade, only to
be pulled up a moment later.

*Give him little pieces of information. Make him
feel like the two of you are going to be each other's
new best friend.... You'll get everything you need.*

"My mother and I live together." She felt as if
she were petting a snake.

"Have you ever been married?"

"No."

His expression shifted subtly, as if she'd given the
right answer to a test question. "Just like me. I'm
not married, either. I'm single," he added as if for
clarification.

Hannah tapped the file on the table before them.
"You told the intake officers you were married."

His lips moved, but the rest of his face didn't. "I
lied."

"And why is that?"

"Because I could."

"Are you as much an expert at that as you are at
building bombs?"

"Not really," he admitted. "Bombs are what I do
best."

"Where did you learn this skill?"

"My father taught me."

Hannah could feel the blood leave her face and for a moment she went numb. Quinn had told her there might be two of them. She asked the first question she could think of to give herself more time. "And how did he learn?"

"He was a miner in Kentucky and he opened the shafts. He always said I'd never be as good as him, but he was wrong." His eyes drilled hers. "Wasn't he? He was wrong...."

Hannah had no choice. "Of course he was wrong," she said. "You're the expert."

He nodded and she breathed. "That's right. I'm the expert."

"Does your father help you now?"

Pinkley's lips twitched again, the rictus somehow more creepy than before. "If he does, it's from hell...because I blew him there ten years back. I celebrate the anniversary of that occasion every other January. It seems to get the New Year off to a good start."

Hannah remembered Quinn's prophecy, a coppery taste filling her mouth as she accidentally bit the inside of her lip.

Pinkley jerked forward again, and this time, it seemed as if he managed to get closer. In fact, if she hadn't known better, she would have sworn he'd touched her. A cold tingle down the side of her neck, a feathery stroke to her cheek, a passing graze against her lips. She held herself rigid in the chair, her only movement, her runaway pulse.

"But I'm not a killer." His eyes were a strange color—a cross between brown and green that reminded her of a scummy pond. "He deserved to die, but he's the only one I've ever hurt. And that's the truth."

"I may have to disagree with you there, Mr. Pinkley. You *are* a killer." Hannah's voice was steady and calm; it hid all the passion she'd felt for months. "In New Orleans, you severely injured a teammate of mine and you murdered two innocent children with one of your devices. I don't know about your father, but these kids certainly didn't deserve to die. If your definition of being a killer demands guilt, you screwed up."

His face flushed red, the line of his jaw going tight with anger. "I didn't kill those kids."

"Well, someone sure did." A montage of painful images flashed through her mind. "I went to their funeral."

"It wasn't me." He strained against his chair. "I did the others—Georgia, Mississippi, South Carolina, Florida—but I did not set that bomb in New Orleans. I swear—"

"We have evidence, Mr. Pinkley."

"Not that links that bombing to me. I didn't do New Orleans." His voice returned to its original chilling flatness, his eyes the same. "And I can prove it."

She looked at him skeptically.

"Call the guard," he said.

She stared at him and his empty eyes. Had there ever been a person behind them? A real, living person who cared about others, who was loved as a child? She didn't think so. She stood up and motioned through the window to the guard.

The uniformed man opened the door and stepped inside. "Yes, ma'am?"

She pointed to the man on the other side of the desk.

Pinkley rattled his handcuffs against his chair. The sound was disconcerting and Hannah winced.

"Take these off," Pinkley commanded. "I want her to see my hands."

CHAPTER TWELVE

To HANNAH'S SURPRISE, the guard complied. "Wasn't no reason to handcuff him to begin with," he said as he reached over and unlocked Pinkley. "He asked me to, so I did."

Hannah looked at the prisoner in confusion. "Why did you ask to be cuffed?"

"I didn't want you to see, but now I guess you have to."

Hannah's heart began to thud, his words sending a chill straight into her heart as he slowly raised his hands. Turning them back and forth before her eyes, he waited for her reaction.

What she saw was so incomprehensible, she didn't understand. When her brain finally managed to master the sight, she gaped. "Oh, my God…"

"Wasn't God what did this to me," he said flatly. "I did it to myself."

She wanted to look away, but she couldn't. On his right hand, he had only two fingers. On his left hand, there were three. The skin was puckered and red, in some places white and slick. The wounds weren't fresh—they'd obviously healed some time ago—but the horrific scars would be with him always.

"Call Martha Miller in Augusta." With a graceful yet sick fluidity, he moved his mangled hands before Hannah's eyes. "She's my cousin and she's a nurse. I couldn't go to the hospital so she took care of me after it happened."

Hannah made the connection with no more prompting. The South Carolina bombing had taken place in a small town east of Augusta.

"You hurt yourself in Bamberg."

"Afterward. I stayed around there for a while to work on something different, but it didn't go right. I *knew* what I was doing," he said defensively. "But I got some bad wire. It shorted and set off my project prematurely. It wasn't my fault."

"Of course not," she agreed. "Of course not."

"But it ended my knotting days. That's why I had to twist the wires in Florida. Took me months just to figure out how to do that. Got me off schedule, too. I should have waited until next January at least, but I got anxious and decided on October instead. I shouldn't have done that. If I'd waited, I wouldn't be here now." His expression was one of genuine distress and Hannah was immediately reminded—again—of Quinn's assessment.

His excuses droned on, but Hannah didn't listen.

The significance of his deformity was registering. The room seemed to shrink, all the air inside going the way of her previous conclusions about the case.

The timing wires on the bomb in New Orleans had been exactly like the wires in all the previous bombings. Georgia. Mississippi. South Carolina. New Orleans. They'd all been perfect duplicates. The wires in *Destin* had been twisted because Pinkley no longer possessed the dexterity required to knot them. He had been injured.

Before the New Orleans bomb.

Hannah swallowed the bile that rose in her throat. Quinn had been right about this, as well. But he'd been wrong, too.

There *was* more than one bomber…but the copycat hadn't done Destin. He'd done New Orleans.

Pinkley's monotone refocused Hannah's attention. "It was easy, but I survived…just like your buddy, Quinn, did—"

He stopped when Hannah's eyes locked on his. "You know Quinn?"

"You bet, I do." He lifted his chin. "I read all about him in the newspaper. He's a hotshot bomb expert. He went into that building and tried to save those kids. He wasn't fast enough, though. He's an expert but I'm better. I would have built a safety timer. That way I would have had some extra time."

A hint of slyness slipped into his expression, a

hint he'd hidden well until this moment. It jarred her. Daniel Pinkley was smarter than he let on.

"I always keep track of my competition," he added, his eyes on her face.

Her skin crawled. "Your competition?" she said carefully. "What do you mean?"

He held out his mangled hands. "He's an expert...I'm an expert. Who's the best?"

"You're crazy" almost slipped out, but she swallowed the words. "You have a point," she said instead, feeling sick inside.

He nodded and smiled. "Who better to set a bomb than someone like him?"

She felt herself recoil, but he continued, her reaction unnoticed.

"You know firemen like to play with fire—I bet the same holds true for guys like him." Again, the slyness slipped into his eyes. "Tell the truth...haven't you ever thought about what it'd be like to blow something sky-high? To watch the flames shoot up and hear the noise and see everybody's face when it goes off? Boom!" He slapped his palms against the table as he spoke.

She jumped despite herself and he laughed.

She cursed silently but recovered fast, her voice sharp. "I think you're forgetting something—why would Quinn set a bomb then run into a building that was going to blow? That'd be stupid and experts aren't stupid, right?''

He raised his hands then dropped them, his gaze going somewhere far away. She could almost hear him thinking. ''Maybe something went wrong. Maybe the timer was off. We all make mistakes.''

''Why do it in the first place?''

''It's the ultimate way to order the world. For once, you're in total control. He's that kind of guy, isn't he?'' He seemed to puff out his chest. ''Too bad he wasn't good enough. I would have set a safety timer and wired it for an outside trip.''

''And the children? What about them—''

''I don't know,'' he interrupted, ''and I don't care. But I didn't do it.'' Leaning closer to the table, he froze her in place. She wanted to cringe, but she couldn't. Then she caught a sudden whiff of something. She needed a second to identify the stringent odor, but after she did, she knew her imagination was playing tricks on her. He couldn't smell like sulfur.

''I didn't kill those kids,'' he hissed. ''I *know* what I'm doing. I'm the expert.''

Hannah forced herself to look into his empty eyes. ''If you didn't murder those children, then who did?''

He put his nightmarish hands on the table. ''I guess you're going to have to do your job and find that out. But if I was you—'' he arched pale eyebrows, and she realized they'd been plucked ''—I'd ask my boyfriend first.''

QUINN'S INTERVIEW WITH Bobby was short and to the point.

''You should have called me, Quinn.'' Sitting behind his expansive desk, Bobby glared at Quinn. ''*Before* you called Washington.''

Quinn shut the door and sat down in one of the chairs. Bobby had replaced all Bill Ford's furniture with larger mahogany pieces. They seemed to take up half the office.

''I did call,'' Quinn said. ''But they told me you were on vacation so I phoned Washington.'' He held out his hands. ''What's the big deal, Bobby? You knew I wanted to come back.''

At Quinn's casual tone, Bobby's broad shoulders relaxed, but it seemed as if it took a lot of effort. ''It's not a big deal,'' he said, ''but it would have been nice to know in advance what your plans were. I only found out because I checked my e-mail while I was gone. I wasn't prepared.''

''There was no need for you to prepare. I've scheduled an appointment with Barroso next week and he'll give me an okay. Then we can change my status from temporary to permanent. That's it.''

Bobby crossed his arms, leaning back in his chair

to stare at Quinn as he spoke. "And what about Hannah?"

"What about her?"

"You haven't forgotten our conversation in the hospital, Quinn. You couldn't have."

"I haven't forgotten it. But I don't think it's relevant anymore. Things have changed."

"They haven't changed that much. Hannah still loves you and she's always going to worry about you." He paused. "Baker already told me you two were together again."

"She won't let that interfere with her job." Quinn explained the meth lab in Destin. "She only made that mistake before because of exhaustion."

"I don't see it that way. And neither do the guys she could have killed that day."

They stared at each other over the desk, Quinn's look steady and calm.

Bobby took a deep breath and got up from his chair, pacing first to his bookcase, then over to the window. He made two round trips and ended up at the glass where he stood in silence. Quinn spoke to his back.

"She's worked the Rogers case like a madman and she's about to break it. You know what she's doing right now, don't you? Who she's talking to?"

"Yes, I know."

"He's already locked up, Bobby, and she's digging the details out of him. The media's been on this one from the beginning, and when they find out she's ended it, they'd crucify you if you sack her.''

''Worse things can happen.''

Quinn felt his jaw tighten. ''I know that. And so do the Williamses. But you can't fire her.''

From across the room, Bobby turned slowly. His gaze never faltered. ''I'm in charge of the team now, Quinn. So I'll be the one who makes that decision, not you.''

A rush of anger came over Quinn at Bobby's words, but he stayed silent. When Bobby said nothing else, Quinn stood and walked out the door.

A little later, parking his truck outside Hannah's bungalow, Quinn sat in the darkness and listened to the call of a cardinal, thinking about the exchange.

The level of tension he'd felt from Baker and Bobby was high, too high. With the case about to break, he would have expected something different. But the two men were like wires drawn so taut they were about to snap. Why was that?

The question only generated more confusion, but in the midst of that, he realized what had been nagging him. Hannah had told him no one's life had really been threatened when she'd dropped the pipe bomb. The Andros had been pointed away from the team. If no one had been in danger, why had Bobby

made Quinn think the opposite for months and even
reiterate the exaggeration tonight?

What in the hell was going on?

HANNAH LEFT THE PRISON in a daze, her thoughts so
tangled she felt as if someone had plucked out her
brain and shaken it, then stuck it back in upside
down. Nothing made sense.

Quinn setting his own bomb? Good God...

She wasn't too sure how she made it back to Destin, but she got herself to the airport and made her
flight. Once onboard, she called Lena's office and
told them where she'd parked the SUV. She promised Bradley Thompson a report, then she leaned
back in her seat and closed her eyes.

Her skin felt oily, her clothes dirty. She knew this
wasn't the case, but talking with Daniel Pinkley
made her feel that way. Opening her eyes, she stared
out at the water beneath the plane. She'd met more
ghouls than she could keep track of, but Daniel
Pinkley was in a category all his own.

And that's what creeped her out the most—because some of the things he'd said made an awful
kind of sense.

She tried not to think about his hints, but her brain
refused to move on. What would Quinn have gained
by setting that bomb? Why would he have done such
a thing? He was fascinated by bombs, but wasn't

she as well? To some degree, wasn't that why they did what they did?

She recalled Quinn's attitude the day of the bombing. He'd been adamant when he'd realized those children were inside, refusing to let anyone else go in. Bobby had tried and Hannah, too, but Quinn had denied the task to both of them, taking total responsibility himself. How come?

She couldn't think of an answer—more questions came instead—and then she thought about the past few weeks.

Out of the blue, Quinn had insinuated himself into the investigation, calling her and asking her to come see him. He'd been "studying" the case all along and had told her there were two bombers. He'd shown up unexpectedly in Destin and questioned Baker's involvement, then he'd helped her with Inlandson. Working together on the meth lab, they'd been drawn even closer.

They'd even made love.

What did it all mean?

She groaned out loud before she could stop herself and the older woman sitting beside her frowned sympathetically.

"I hate to fly, too," she said. "It's scary, isn't it?"

Hannah gave her a weak smile and turned back

to the window. Her *life* was scary, she thought. And totally out of control.

She let her thoughts run rampant until the plane landed. As she inched down the aisle with everyone else, then made her way through the almost deserted terminal and to the parking garage, Hannah decided things might be crazy, but at least she'd managed to accomplish her objective. She'd left that jail with Pinkley's confession to all the bombings except New Orleans, and that was pretty damn good. Quinn himself couldn't have done any better.

The unexpected thought triggered a surprising discovery: She'd always compared herself to Quinn, and now Hannah realized what a mistake that had been. They were each very good, but in very different ways. She'd managed Pinkley's interview perfectly, but she hadn't enjoyed it. She still preferred sitting at her desk, studying the bits and pieces men like him left behind. She could do the other and do it well—she no longer had to prove that fact, to herself or anyone else—but why continue on that path if there was another one available?

She rejoined the crowd and headed to the parking lot. She had some thinking to do.

HANNAH'S CELL PHONE RANG just as she merged onto the freeway. Driving with one hand, she picked up the phone with the other. "Crosby."

"Hannah, it's Mark. Where are you?"

"I'm on the freeway. I just got in from Destin—"

"Bobby told me you were talking to a suspect."

"Not just a suspect," she said grimly. "You aren't going to believe—"

He completely ignored her startling words. "I need to see you. Can you meet me at my house?"

Hannah blinked. "Didn't you hear what I said? You'll have to come to the office if you want—"

"No! Come to my house *right now*. It's important, Hannah, or I wouldn't ask you to do this, I promise."

Quinn's warnings about Mark's behavior echoed in her head. "I don't want to go to your house, Mark. If you've got something to tell me, tell me now."

"It's too complicated." Desperation edged its way into his voice. "I'm not shitting you, Hannah. This is for real. But I can't explain over the phone and I sure as hell can't tell you at the office. And for God's sake, don't tell anyone there about this."

"Mark, I—"

"It's about the New Orleans bombing," he continued. "If you really want to solve that case, then you need to come talk to me."

She paused. "What makes you think I didn't close it by talking to my suspect?"

Silence from Mark, then he said, "I know you

didn't…because I know who really set that bomb. Get over here and I'll prove it."

Then he hung up.

A passing truck sounded his horn and Hannah sucked in a gasp. Concentrating on Mark's crazy statement, she'd allowed her car to weave out of its lane. Jerking the vehicle to where it should be, she thought about it for another mile, then she exited the freeway and headed for Mark's house. Grabbing her phone, she started to punch the numbers to the office. She needed someone to know where she was going.

But she dialed the first three digits, then stopped. Mark had told her not to tell anyone at the office. And Quinn had warned her about Mark! She didn't want to worry her mother and Quinn didn't even have a cell phone. Her head spinning, Hannah cleared the phone and dialed again. Her own voice answered.

"You've reached the desk of Hannah Crosby. Please leave your message at the tone."

"It's me, Hannah," she said, feeling foolish as she talked to her own machine. "I'm leaving this message in case…in case something goes wrong. I'm on my way to Mark's house because he just called me and said he knows something about the New Orleans bombing." She glanced at her watch. "It's almost 11:00 p.m."

A second of silence ticked by, and she thought about Quinn. Thought about leaving a message for him, too. Thought about everything that had happened between the two of them and everything that had yet to be decided. Could they ever come to an agreement on their differences? Their future was one of those things she needed to think about some more, so she simply hung up.

Thirty minutes later she pulled up in front of Mark Baker's house. From behind drawn shades, lights seemed to be on in almost every room. Hannah wanted to drive away, but instead she climbed from the car and started up the sidewalk.

QUINN LEFT THE SANCTUARY of his truck and made his way to Hannah's front door. Deep in thought, he pressed the bell and waited.

A few minutes later, Barbara Crosby opened the door. Her smile was genuine as she looked up at Quinn.

"Quinn! It's great to see you. Please, come in, come in...."

He stepped inside the gleaming entry and bent down to envelop Barbara in his arms. That's when he noticed the other woman standing in the nearby living room. Barbara hugged him tightly, then stepped back.

"Hello, Lindsey," he said. "It's good to see you

again. Hope things are going well for you." He took the woman's hand and gently squeezed it, noting the look Barbara and her best friend exchanged. No doubt, his and Hannah's relationship had been a topic of conversation between the two of them.

"Come sit down," Barbara invited. "We have a lot of catching up to do."

"I'd like to do that," he said, following her into the living room, "but before we get started, is Hannah back yet?"

"No, she hasn't made it in." Barbara glanced down at her watch, then back up at him. "She was on a late flight, wasn't she?"

"She was, but she should have come in by now. She promised she'd let me know when she got here and we'd get together." He tilted his head toward the phone at the end of the sofa. "I'll call and see what's going on. She might have gotten stuck in Destin."

The two women left him alone. Hannah's cell rang forever, but the airline's answer was quick. The flight had arrived on time. Quinn called Lena next, and she picked up on the second ring.

"It's Quinn." He didn't waste time on preliminaries. "Did you hear from Hannah before she left there?"

"Yes, we did. She called in from the plane and talked to Bradley."

"That flight takes four, maybe five hours, right?"

"That's correct. It's not a direct route." Lena's voice was no-nonsense. "What's up? Is there something going on I need to know about?"

"I don't think so," Quinn answered. "But I haven't heard from her yet. I'll be in touch."

For reasons he couldn't explain, Quinn remembered the air of unease that had hung over the office. Something was going on with Mark and Bobby.

Interrupting his thoughts, Barbara and Lindsey entered the living room, each carrying a tray, one covered with a teapot, cups and saucers, the other holding enough sandwiches to feed a crowd at the Superdome.

Barbara put down her tray, took one look at his face, then straightened her back as if bracing herself. "What's wrong?"

"Nothing that I know of...but no one seems to know where Hannah is and I need to talk to her about the case before I can do anything else. I'm sorry, but I better go back to the office. Have her call me if she gets in."

Barbara walked outside. He looked down at her and suffered a start; he'd forgotten her eyes were just like Hannah's.

"Is my daughter all right?" she asked.

Quinn put his hand on Barbara's arm. The bones beneath his fingers felt more fragile than he'd expected—she always seemed so strong and in control, it surprised him to think of her as vulnerable in any way. But she was. They all were. If he'd learned anything from his accident, it was that.

He patted her arm. "I'm sure she's fine, Barbara. She probably got caught up in something and turned off her phone so she could concentrate."

"My daughter needs you, Quinn. And you need her. When are the two of you going to accept that?"

Quinn tried to gentle his voice. "It's not that simple, Barbara."

"Yes, it is."

"She wants things I don't."

Her gaze went sharp. "That's an excuse, and you know it. Everyone wants children, a home, marriage. And so do you. But it scares you half to death."

He stared at her in surprise. "I don't want a family because of our jobs. We can't have kids while Hannah and I are doing what we do. It's too damn dangerous."

She made a scoffing sound. "That's ridiculous. Do you actually think life comes with guarantees? With thirty-day promises? If that's what you're waiting for, then you're in big trouble—"

"Considering my job and everything I've been through, I think I should know what to expect—"

"That's right, you should," she interrupted. "So

that brings us back to the real problem, doesn't it? You're scared.''

He decided to humor her. ''And what exactly is it that I'm scared of, Barbara?''

''Of loving my daughter...then losing her.'' She narrowed her eyes and stared him down. ''You're terrified that what happened to you might happen to her and then you'd be alone with only the memory of what you two shared. The hell of it is—that's all you're going to have, anyway, if you don't set this straight.''

She waited for his reply, but he couldn't think of anything to say. And she knew it.

She nodded in satisfaction, stepped back inside the house and closed the door behind her.

CHAPTER THIRTEEN

HANNAH MADE HER WAY up the sidewalk with slow and deliberate steps. Mark Baker was not an idiot. If he was setting her up, anything could be rigged, from the doorbell to the fern on the porch. She flashed back for a second to the meth lab. She'd spotted the rug in front of the trailer, but only after she'd seen Quinn's eyes on it first. His sixth sense had really saved them. Not having a skill even close to that, all Hannah could do was concentrate.

Focusing on everything, she reached the porch, then stopped abruptly as a metal glint beneath one of the balusters caught her eye. She froze, every muscle tensing.

What was it? A trip wire? A pressure device? A timer?

Peering into the darkness, she stared until the form of a crumpled soda can emerged. Anyone else might have been relieved.

She took a step closer and slowly bent down, her elbows on her knees, her gaze intense. After a moment, she released the breath she'd been holding.

The can had probably been there for days, she decided, an uneven but steady line of ants going from the sticky metal lip to the edge of the porch. She stood up and returned to the front door, avoiding the oval window set in the center and the mat beneath.

She counted slowly to five and listened, every nerve on full alert. The neighborhood was an older one just off the freeway, and she could hear the rumbling traffic from where she stood. No sounds at all came from inside the house. Her eyes went to the yellow gleam of a doorbell button just to her left, but she decided to knock instead. Her knuckles were a breath away when the door opened unexpectedly.

She bit back a scream, her heart leaping into her throat and lodging itself there.

"Shit, Baker! You scared me half to death!" Her hand on her chest, she stared wide-eyed at the man on the threshold. "I was just about to—"

Without a word, he grabbed her arm and pulled her inside. The door slammed behind them as Hannah stumbled then caught herself, yanking her arm free from his grip. "What the hell—"

His shirt was untucked, his jeans rumpled. He looked as if he'd been drinking, but she could smell no liquor on him. She smelled something, though, and as he spoke, she recognized that it was fear.

"Does anyone know you came here?" He looked past her to the window, his eyes darting as he lifted the sheer drapery to stare outside before dropping it a second later. "Did you tell anyone at the office?"

She hesitated and wondered which was best—to let him know she might be missed or to try to gain his trust. "I didn't tell anyone, but my mother's expecting me shortly," she finally said. "What's going on, Mark? You look like a madman and you're acting crazy...."

He laughed, then cut off the sound a moment later. "I'm crazy all right," he said. "You will be, too, when I tell you what I've found out."

"Tell me."

"Not here." He glanced behind her again. "Come into the den. I don't want to stand by the window. Someone could see..."

Before she could ask who that someone might be, Mark tugged her into the room at their right. It was a study of sorts, a desk in one corner, a lamp sitting on the edge of it. Two lawn chairs were in the opposite corner. The window behind them was covered with a shade, but in front of it, he'd hung a sheet, as well. Could it get any weirder?

"You went to see Mr. Rogers today, right?" His voice was strained and tight.

"I saw a guy who claims he is," Hannah said slowly. "His name is Daniel Pinkley—"

"What'd he tell you?"

She looked at the tech with a calmness she didn't

feel. "I'm not saying a thing until you explain what you said to me on the phone."

He stared at her and licked his lips, his eyes darting from her face to the windows and back. Any suspicion she'd had that Mark himself had been involved with the bombings fled. He was scared out of his mind. "Pinkley told you he didn't do New Orleans, didn't he?"

She hedged. "They all say they didn't do it, Mark. You know that."

"Yeah, they do." He blinked and seemed to focus. "But in this case, he's telling the truth."

THE BULLPEN WAS EMPTY and silent as Quinn entered and headed directly to Hannah's desk. All the way from her house to here, he'd been hoping he'd walk into the room and see her sitting there, but he'd known she wouldn't be. A bad feeling was growing inside him. A very bad feeling. Pulling out her empty chair, he cursed his intuition for being powerful enough to sense the danger but not powerful enough to figure out where she might be.

He began to study her desk. The brown plants on either corner were anchors for numerous files and papers. It looked messy, but Hannah had her own system. She could find anything anyone might need in seconds. He opened her center drawer and looked for the notebook she usually carried, but as he expected, it wasn't there. She probably had it with her. He found more files, two tubes of lipstick and a small bottle of aspirin, but no notebook.

Slamming the drawer so hard the desk rattled, Quinn suddenly noticed the blinking light on Hannah's phone. She had a message. Without hesitation, he punched in the PIN she consistently used. She proved as predictable in this case as she was with everything else, and Quinn blessed her silently. The message played back.

The minute he heard her voice his heart started a painful pounding that only served to scare him more.

"It's me, Hannah. I'm leaving this message in case…in case something goes wrong. I'm on my way to Mark's house because he just called me and said he knows something about the New Orleans bombing. It's almost 11:00 p.m."

He stood so fast, he almost fell, the pain in his thigh shooting up and into his hip. He gasped and grabbed his leg but he didn't stop. Running out of the office, he pretended he was all right and prayed that Hannah was.

HANNAH'S THROAT CONSTRICTED at Mark's announcement, the awful taste of fear filling her mouth. In a voice that didn't sound like her own, she asked, "Who did it?"

He didn't hesitate. "It was Bobby, Hannah. Bobby Justice. He set the whole thing up."

"Bobby! God, you are crazy." She would have laughed if Mark's expression had been less frightened, but as it was, she couldn't. He was clearly petrified. She stood up, all her suspicions flooding back. Was he trying to throw her off? "Tell me why you think that," she demanded.

"Remember that file you told me to find? The one about the Mississippi case?"

"You never found it."

"I did find it, but not until a few days ago. It was in Bobby's desk drawer. I broke into his office and found it there."

"You broke into his office?" Hannah stared at the tech in dismay. "Good grief, Mark, why didn't you just ask him about the file? He was probably reviewing it again. I've done that, you've done that…it doesn't mean anything—"

"Hannah, he took the file without checking it out. I saw him putting it back and got suspicious because he was acting so weird about it."

"So he forgot to sign for it—big deal—"

Mark interrupted. "No. He'd taken it so he could copy it, Hannah. The file I found in his desk was a duplicate. He'd made all kinds of notes on it."

Copying files was against EXIT's rules. In an investigation one record—and only one—was kept of all the important information, to avoid any confusion. But still… Hannah stared at Mark in disbelief. "This is your proof?"

"No." Mark shook his head, his jaw tightening. "That's not my proof."

"What else?"

"He had the recipe, too."

The room fell silent as Hannah absorbed Mark's words. A list of ingredients was developed for every device that EXIT encountered, and Hannah alone was in charge of that procedure. As she analyzed the debris of each investigation, she developed a recipe of sorts that named the explosives used in the making of the bomb, along with all the other pertinent details, including the necessary amounts of all the materials and step-by-step directions.

No one accessed the cookbook without her consent. She kept it under lock and key. "How did he—"

"I don't know how he got it, but it was there. Along with the recipes for Georgia and South Carolina."

She tried to follow through with logic—it was all she had left since nothing else made any sense. "But even if he had the recipe, he couldn't duplicate the devices. He'd have to have the right materials, too."

"He's got them."

Her blood turned to ice, chilly fingers tapping down her spine. "How do you know that?"

"I searched his house while he was on vacation and I found a receipt to a storage unit. I traced it to a place over on Highway 90, almost to Boutte." He stopped.

"And you discovered..."

"His shop."

Hannah blinked, her brain unable to assimilate Mark's words. Every bomber had a hole—their shop—where they went to make their bombs. Preparing their devices where they lived was too dangerous.

"He had all the tools, Hannah. And a stash of RDX. And knotted wires." He scrubbed his face with his hands, then looked up at her. "He had one of those magnifying glasses with a light on it—you know, like the one you use to study fragments. It was set up on a desk. There were little piles of tied wires all over the place. He'd been practicing."

Her mouth fell open; she couldn't help it.

"I took samples of his mix and had it tested on my own. The combination is identical." He took a shaky breath. "He had to have done it, Hannah. It's the only conclusion that makes any sense. I've been scared to death to tell anyone until I was sure, and then when I decided I *was* sure, I was even more scared."

Hannah nodded, the questions overwhelming. Why had he done it? What was going on? She remembered the look in his eyes when they'd found out the Williams children were inside—he'd seemed genuinely horrified. Had that been an act or for real?

She blinked and tried to clear her mind, Mark's anxious eyes on her face. A plan began to form, but she had to verify Mark's evidence before doing anything else. They'd both look like idiots if what he had wasn't rock solid. "I have to see what you've found," she said. "Then we'll go from there."

He nodded eagerly. "I hid the reports and RDX in the garage." He tilted his head toward the back of the house. "Come on. I'll show you."

QUINN BARELY TAPPED his brakes as he headed out of the parking garage and onto the street. Mark Baker's house was twenty minutes from the office, but Quinn made it in ten.

The second he took the corner onto Baker's street, he spotted Hannah's car. The red Mustang sat directly in front, right by the curb. He kept driving and passed the home and vehicle. When he reached the end of the block, he turned and parked out of sight. He didn't know what was going on, and until he did he wanted surprise on his side. Sprinting back down the street, he crouched behind her right front fender, reaching upward to touch the hood of the

Mustang. The metal was still warm, but just barely. She'd been there for some time.

Quinn peered around the corner of the car and studied Baker's house. Light came from every window—the place was obviously occupied—yet the home had an air of strange emptiness.

With growing uneasiness, he sent quick glances to the homes on either side. Both were dark and silent, their wooden fences bordering the one around Baker's back yard. Because the street lamp was nearest to the right one, Quinn picked the house on the left and sprinted toward the fence. Within seconds, he was over it and peering through the slats to Baker's backyard.

It was empty.

Grasping the edge of the nearest slat, Quinn pulled himself to the top of the seven-foot fence and dropped to the ground beside Baker's air-conditioning unit. He hit hard and twisted wrong, a cold, hard pain rippling up his leg. The unexpected agony made him gasp out loud, but the humming motor of the air-conditioning unit covered the sound. Gritting his teeth, he immediately rolled behind the metal box for cover. When he'd regained his breath, he inched his way toward the house.

HANNAH HESITATED, BUT ONLY for a second. Mark was telling the truth and she knew it. The instinctive realization shocked her—she wasn't supposed to have that ability. Yet, she knew—knew for certain—that he was being honest with her.

She gave him a quick nod, then followed him through the house. The living room was as sparse as the study in the front, the kitchen even more so. As they stepped through a widened hall that did double duty as a laundry room, Hannah felt an unexpected flash of sympathy for the man in front of her. His demeanor was always so brazen and obnoxious, she'd never really thought about who he actually was. If his house was any indication, Mark Baker was a lonely person. There were no photos of any kind, no personal mementos of a family or even a life other than his work. She wanted to ask him about the brother he'd told Quinn he had, but now was definitely not the time for that.

Through a square window in the center of the door, she saw a short covered walkway that led directly to a detached garage. The garage door itself faced the street, but access could also be gained through a single door set off to one side. To the left of the sidewalk and that door, there was a small patio, the bare concrete gleaming in the darkness. Mark opened the back door and headed straight to the one that led into the garage.

Hannah had always heard that things went into

slow motion during a catastrophe, but that's not how it worked.

As Mark approached the garage, everything sped up. Hannah saw the door, she saw the beam, she saw the glimmer of a short silver box.

But her warning came too late.

Mark couldn't stop in time.

The forward motion of his right leg broke the line of light. A split second later, the bomb went off.

HER FEET LEFT THE GROUND, and a heartbeat after that Hannah was flying backward, past Baker's washer and dryer. When she saw a refrigerator and a stove, she realized she'd been blown at least twelve feet, but that was all that registered. Debris came at her from every direction, taking what was left of her attention. Pieces of the roof, a doorknob, an empty ice cooler, even something that looked like part of a car.

A stinging nettle of broken glass peppered her face and then she slammed into something that didn't move. A shock wave of pain rolled over her and her breath left her chest in a whoosh. She *felt* the cracking sound that followed as something inside her snapped. *Bones,* she thought through a torturous haze, most likely her ribs. For one quick second she thought of Quinn and all he meant to her.... Then she gave up and let the darkness take her.

THE EXPLOSION WAS DEAFENING. Literally.

Quinn heard the bomb go off and he ducked, but after that, his world went quiet, a painful deafness instantly in place. He cursed the vacuum of sound and covered his head with his arms, the house offering little protection against the shrapnel that flew in his direction. He gasped for air, the terror of the day-care explosion echoing in his brain.

Jumping up before the rain of debris even finished, Quinn ran through the smoke toward the back of the house. Flames were already moving up what was left of the walls.

His training took over, but accompanying it was horror.

Baker—or what was left of him—was past help.

And Hannah had disappeared.

A flood of bile rose to his throat. Quinn fought it, frantically searching the now devastated backyard and patio. There was no sight of her. For a moment too long to live through, he thought the worst, then he realized what had happened. The force of the blast had thrown her back into the house.

And under a mountain of rubble.

CHAPTER FOURTEEN

HE SHOULD HAVE CALLED for backup. He should have looked for secondaries. He should have waited for help.

But Quinn did none of those things.

He rushed headlong into what was left of Baker's home, his only concern Hannah.

He frantically dug through broken wooden beams, crushed wallboard and fragments of furniture, screaming Hannah's name. He realized his hearing was returning when he heard flames crackling behind him, the heat of the explosion sweeping into the ruins of the house, the tattered draperies and carpet serving as fuel. Noxious fumes accompanied the fire, the smell of burning plastic stinging Quinn's eyes and lungs. He coughed violently and started to gag, bending over abruptly.

And that's when he saw a glimmer of pink.

He struggled to recall what Hannah had chosen to wear that morning in the hotel in Destin, but his mind wouldn't focus. Instead of eighteen hours, it seemed as if a year had passed since that time.

Then he remembered. She'd misbuttoned the blouse.

And it *had* been pink.

He fell to his knees and began to dig while in the distance, the sound of sirens penetrated the noise behind him. Ten frantic seconds passed before he was sure he'd found her. As he raised the last splintered board, his leg threatened to collapse...but it was his heart that actually stopped working.

Hannah's unmoving form lay before him, her torso twisted, her arms flung out in an unnatural angle. Her hair was darkened with soot and dust, her clothing filthy and torn. The cuts that crisscrossed her face were mostly superficial, but a larger, more serious slash above her right eye was already swelling, the stream of blood a steady one.

Quinn fell to his knees beside her, then frantically ripped off his shirt to stem the flow. After bandaging the wound as best he could, he moved on to her arms and legs, running his hands over them all. Her limbs seemed intact, but when he reached her left side and pressed, she gave a moan that made him wince.

A few moments later the first fireman reached Quinn. The guy was a veteran named Alberto Brown, and Quinn and Hannah both had known him for years. When he looked down, his eyes filled with surprise. "Good God! Is that who I think it is? We thought this was a regular fire call! You guys involved with this?''

Quinn jerked his head to the men already unloading their gear behind him. ''For God's sake, get them out of here, Al. There may be secondary devices, more UXO—''

He didn't have to repeat himself. The possibility of unexploded ordnance jerked Brown into action. He screamed at the firefighters and waved them back. Quinn heard someone else yell ''EXIT,'' and then the scramble was on.

Only Brown stayed put. He bent down and began to pull Quinn away. ''We need to load and go, Quinn. Get out of the way so I can get to her.''

It was SOP to remove injured bombing victims as soon as possible, then search for more devices. But it wasn't SOP for the woman he loved to be the injured one. Quinn hesitated, then realized he could be making a fatal mistake.

He jumped out of the way and Brown waved the medics over. When they had Hannah secure, Quinn moved closer and helped as the medics put a collar on her neck and moved her onto the board. The men then carried her to the waiting ambulance, stepping their way over the wreckage, Quinn following before climbing inside the vehicle.

The white van pulled away from the curb seconds later, painting the neighborhood with flashing red lights as Quinn sat at Hannah's side, his hands clasping hers. A black blur momentarily distracted him. He glanced out the back window in time to see an EXIT SUV swing into the spot the ambulance had been parked in seconds before.

Bobby climbed from the vehicle, his yellow EXIT jacket standing out against the lights.

Quinn turned back to Hannah and bent his head to hers, his heart keeping time with the siren's warning cries.

WHEN THE AMBULANCE ARRIVED at Charity Hospital, Quinn felt as if he'd fallen through a hole and slipped backward in time. They were repeating the events of the previous January, but in reverse—Hannah on the stretcher, him crazy with fear.

The surreal intensity continued as the nurses took Hannah through the hospital hallways, Quinn running alongside. At some point, two doctors joined them. With the gurney still in motion, they began their examination, barking out orders while the growing entourage flew through the corridors. They burst through one set of double doors, and then another. Finally, everyone stopped. Quinn was pushed to one side and told to leave.

But Hannah had come to. Crying out, she tried to grab Quinn. Her fingers brushed his jacket, then fell away as she gasped from the effort. He stepped around the nearest nurse and grabbed Hannah's hand, bending over so she could see him.

"I'm here, baby." He clutched her fingers. "I'm here...."

She pulled him closer with a weak tug, the exertion clearly draining what little strength she had left. He leaned down, but she spoke so hoarsely, he couldn't understand the words.

"It's okay." He tried to reassure her with a soft squeeze of her fingers, but on the inside he was shaking. "You're at the hospital. They're going to take care of you." He repeated the mantra again for himself as much as for her. "You're going to be just fine, I promise."

She spoke again and then again. The third time, he understood.

"Don't..." The words died. Then with a herculean effort, she gathered herself and tried one more time. "Go...back..." she whispered, her voice raw and thick. "Go back...to Mark's house."

"I'm not going anywhere." Quinn used the pledge to warn the nurse who had already ordered him to leave once. She took one look at him and stepped back. He refocused on Hannah. "I'm staying right here. Don't worry."

"You have to move, sir." Another of the nurses, bigger and braver, spoke sharply to him. "We have to get to her—"

Quinn tried to pull away but Hannah wouldn't let him go. She gripped his hand with amazing strength. "Don't stay with *me*," she rasped. "Go...go back to Mark's...before Bobby can get there."

He frowned. "Bobby's there already. He came just as we drove—"

Shocking him with her ferocity, she clenched his hand so hard it hurt. "You. Go. Back. Right now." She gritted her teeth and took a shallow breath. "Mark had proof. Bobby..."

"Bobby what?"

She started to answer, but one of the orderlies forced his way between the two of them. He was taller than Quinn and outweighed him by fifty pounds. "Out of the way, sir. We need to get to work."

Quinn started to argue, but the orderly placed a hand on his shoulder and spoke, the finality of his words too frightening for Quinn to ignore.

"If you don't step away and let us help your friend, she could die. Right here. Right now." He squeezed Quinn's shoulder gently. "You have to leave. The doc will come and get you when he can."

Quinn nodded and followed the man outside the double doors to a row of plastic chairs. He sat down heavily, Hannah's confusing words disturbing him. What "proof" could Mark have had about Bobby?

Quinn puzzled over the words until the orderly returned.

He held out a blue scrub shirt. "This is for you. Guess you lost yours somewhere along the way tonight."

Quinn nodded his thanks, then slipped the shirt on as the man waited. "I won't bother them," Quinn said, tilting his head to the area they'd just left. "You can go."

The white-garbed man spoke softly. "You can go, too, brother. It's gonna take hours to fix your lady."

Quinn started to nod, then all at once he froze, a sudden realization paralyzing him. He cursed once, then jumped to his feet and ran down the hall.

HANNAH SENSED THE PRESENCE of the crowd surrounding her gurney. Drifting in and out, she suffered the painful prods that accompanied the doctor's orders, but most of the turmoil didn't register. A curious detachment enveloped her. She called out for Quinn and tried to raise her hand, but someone hushed her and placed her fingers back on the sheet.

Hannah protested. She had something she had to tell him. It was important. Really important.

The jab of a needle momentarily distracted her. She yelped and tried to jerk away, but the effort was pointless. Whoever had the needle was still holding on to her, preventing her from moving.

They didn't understand. She had to warn Quinn. She had to make sure he knew. She had tell him…something. Out of nowhere, a fog rolled into her brain. She closed her eyes and her body shut down.

QUINN HAD TO GET A RIDE and he knew exactly where the fastest one would be.

Skidding down the polished corridors, he headed straight for the emergency room, reaching it in seconds, despite his leg. Sure enough, a cop leaned against a wall, writing something in a tiny notebook.

Quinn grabbed him and explained. The officer, who looked young enough to be in high school, nodded. A second later, they were in a black and white, speeding back to Mark Baker's house.

"I need your cell phone." Quinn held out his hand and the officer obliged, Quinn's tone giving him no other option.

Barbara answered on the first ring and Quinn explained the best he could. Her voice quivered as she spoke, but beneath it was the same steel that made Hannah so strong.

"I'll be right there," she said. "What floor is she on?"

He told her. "I'm on my way back to the scene, Barbara. They said the doctor would come out when he was finished. Would you call me when he does that?''

''Absolutely.''

He gave her the cop's number, then she spoke again. ''Don't worry about her, Quinn. You go do what you have to do. It's what Hannah would want.''

He agreed, then ended the call, slipping the cop's phone into his pocket without apology. ''I'll get it back to you,'' he promised.

They pulled up to what was left of Baker's house shortly after that.

Despite the lateness of the hour, the crowd was large. The scene had been roped off and lights brought in. There were more cops and more fire trucks, and TV crews were setting up for remote broadcasts.

Quinn jumped from the patrol unit and slammed the door. With a sweeping glance, he took in the devastation, then the two officers guarding the boundaries. They quickly lifted the tape for him to pass, obviously recognizing his EXIT status.

He found Bobby at the back of the house.

He was sifting through the still-smoking debris on the edge of the blast seat, but lifted his head as Quinn rounded the corner.

The minute their gazes connected, Quinn knew everything.

CHAPTER FIFTEEN

"Why?" Anger mixed with shock in Quinn's voice. "Why'd you do it?"

Bobby's expression was pained. "I had to stop them."

A cold fire built inside Quinn's chest. "Stop who?" he asked, knowing the answer already. "From doing what?"

Bobby looked at Quinn and made a sound that might have been a chuckle in another situation. "Ain't that something? You're the one with the special intuition and you never figured it out...."

Quinn took two steps and grabbed Bobby by the collar. He wanted to throw him against the nearest wall, but he shook him instead. "That's me, all right," he growled. "But I want to hear it from you, you son of a bitch."

Bobby's eyes widened in surprise, and for a minute, Quinn thought he might try to get a punch off. Quinn would have liked that. It would have given him all the excuse he needed to start pummeling his friend.

But instead of trying to hit Quinn, Bobby crumpled. Quinn was forced to release his shirt and Bobby almost fell.

"I made the New Orleans bomb, Quinn. I copied Mr. Rogers's signature and set the box myself. I even called it in to LaCroix's team."

Even though he'd expected the words, Quinn's reaction was deep and swift and it almost took him under. He tasted blood in his mouth and realized he'd bit his cheek. "You killed those kids."

Bobby's face twisted. "I didn't know about them! That part was an accident. You don't understand—"

"I don't understand?" Quinn's emotions took over and he got back in Bobby's face. Thumping the other man's chest, Quinn let his anger erupt. "I guess this nine-inch scar I've got is getting in the way of my thinking. Or, no, wait... Maybe it's the fact that my career is over and the pain isn't!" His jaw was clenched so tightly he could hear his teeth grinding together. "Maybe I don't understand because the woman I love is lying in the hospital right now fighting for her life! What do you think, Bobby? You think that's it?"

Bobby held his hand up and stopped the flow of words. "I didn't mean to hurt anyone, and I especially didn't mean to kill those kids."

"Who did you mean to kill? Just me?"

Bobby shook his head, then he sat down abruptly

on the remains of what had once been a workbench. "I didn't plan on killing anybody. You know as well as I do, no one had any idea those kids would be in there." He lifted his eyes. "I just wanted to show them they'd picked the wrong guy…."

Quinn couldn't take in the implication of Bobby's words. The idea was so ludicrous. "For God's sake, man, tell me this isn't about the damn promotion. Tell me that's not the truth."

"It was more than that." Bobby's lips tightened and for the first time anger entered his voice. "You don't have a clue about the crap I've taken over the years."

"You haven't taken any crap from me. Don't even try to sell that shit to me—"

"Maybe not intentionally," Bobby conceded. "But it's been there, even from you. You with your intuition and your 'feelings' about everything…." His face hardened. "I'm just as good a tech as the rest of you. I've done my job and done it well, but no one noticed. They saw you and they saw Hannah, hell, they even saw Baker, but I never counted. I was just the *black* tech. That's it."

"That's bullshit. If it were the case, you wouldn't have gotten the position after I left."

Bobby looked up. "I know that. *Now*…"

Quinn could only shake his head at the enormity

of the waste. He made a sound of disgust. "So you just decided to get rid of all of us?"

"No. That's not what I intended. Things got out of control."

"What in the hell does that mean?"

Bobby looked down at his dusty boots. "I copied Mr. Rogers and set up the New Orleans situation. My plan was to get there first and disrupt the device on my own. You know—look good, be the hero." He glanced at Quinn, his eyes swimming. "I needed that promotion, man. Janie was about to leave and take the kids. She'd seen the shit I'd taken and said no self-respecting man would put up with it. She's always comparing me to those damn lawyers she works with. I decided she was right."

"So you built a bomb and killed two kids."

"I had no idea they'd be in there. After that, things just snowballed."

"Where'd you get the materials? How'd you know the recipe?"

"I stole the RDX from the evidence room." He dropped his eyes. "And I took the recipe from Hannah's cookbook. When Baker realized what was going on, I knew he'd tell her, but I had no idea she'd find the real Mr. Rogers before then. I thought I'd taken care of that possibility when I got you to leave. I—I didn't think Hannah would pursue the guy like she has."

''And you didn't care who else got killed? You didn't care that a serial bomber would still be out there somewhere?''

''I didn't...think about it,'' Bobby answered. ''But Hannah wouldn't turn loose of it. So I had to handle the situation—and her. I planted evidence in my office and made sure Baker knew about it.''

''So when she finally figured out Mr. Rogers didn't do New Orleans, you were going to blame them both.''

Bobby nodded.

''How'd you know it would be tonight?''

''I had her phone tapped. She called and left a message for herself—''

''And you rigged everything then?''

''I had everything ready. It only took a few minutes.'' He swallowed. ''I jumped the other side of the fence seconds before you came into the yard.''

A long moment passed. One of the longest in Quinn's life. Words didn't seem adequate for what he had to express. ''I thought you were my friend,'' he said slowly as he met Bobby's eyes. ''I trusted you with my life. I listened when you told me to quit the team...when you seemed concerned about Hannah. I gave up everything because I thought I needed to...'' Quinn took a deep breath and blew it out. "So much for intuition! How could I have been so blind?"

"You weren't blind. You love her. You did what you had to. Hannah would have sacrificed the same for you."

Quinn stepped closer, and with satisfaction he watched Bobby flinch. "You can't begin to understand what's between Hannah and me so don't tell me what she would have done." Quinn's hands fisted. "In fact, you aren't even fit to speak her name. Say it again and I'll kill you myself."

"LEAVE YOUR GEAR." Quinn tilted his head toward the black leather jacket lying at the edge of the garage. "Evidence can pick it up. I'm going to take you to Central myself."

Bobby nodded, as Quinn pulled his wrists together and cuffed him.

Walking away, Quinn took the cop's cell phone from his pocket and called the office to request backup. Then he punched in the hospital's number and had Barbara paged. She answered a second later.

"Any word?"

"Nothing so far. Is everything all right with you?"

"I'm wrapping things up," he answered obliquely.

"I understand. We'll see you when we see you."

Quinn ended the call and walked back to where Bobby waited by the garage, a growing group of cops and firefighters standing in the driveway. Word had spread. Bobby held his own cell phone, which had been clipped to his belt. "Can I call Janie, Quinn? Once we get downtown, things are gonna get crazy. I—I don't want her to hear about this on the news. Fox-8 is on the curb out front. For God's sake—"

Quinn's anger eased at Bobby's pitiful words. "Okay, okay." He lifted his hand. "Call her. But that's it. Nobody else."

Bobby's expression lightened, his gratefulness embarrassing to Quinn. "Thanks, Quinn. I really appreciate it—"

"Make your call," Quinn instructed harshly. "Then we'll go to Central."

Bobby nodded once and stepped away from Quinn, walking toward the only corner of Baker's garage still standing as he punched in the number.

Then Quinn realized what Bobby was doing.

Quinn sprinted forward, screaming for the crews to scatter. He was three feet away when Bobby hit the send key. He tried to run, but Quinn tackled him and ripped the phone from his hand, heaving it toward the rubble behind them.

Quinn's momentum took them straight to the ground, where he covered Bobby as best he could, using his back and legs to protect the man who'd almost killed him. The explosion sounded and the earth shifted…one more time.

THE BLAST WAVE RIPPLED OUT, the smaller, less-powerful device dissipating its energy in a wide but weak path. Bobby had made the bomb for one purpose and one purpose only. To kill himself. The load packed inside the phone was smaller, the detonator controlled by radio frequency.

The shrapnel had no serious impact, either. The nails and broken pieces of metal fell harmlessly into the ruins of Baker's house, the concussion absorbed by the destruction already there.

With an angry expletive, Quinn got to his knees and yanked Bobby up with him, turning him roughly so they faced each other squarely.

"*Are you finished?* Is there anything else you want to destroy or was that it?" Quinn cursed again, a red curtain of anger sweeping over him as he cocked his fist and started to swing.

It took three men to pull him away.

OVER THE NEXT TWO DAYS, Quinn sat by Hannah's side in the hospital. She drifted in and out of sleep, some natural, most of it drug-induced. He was afraid—even though he knew it made no sense—that she might stop breathing if he looked away. The doctors tried to tell him he'd been much worse off and that she would be fine, but Quinn had a hard time believing them. The bruises on her body were too painful to contemplate. And where she wasn't discolored, she was bandaged. The cut on her forehead had required a dozen stitches and there was another one on her back that was equally bad. But her broken ribs were her most serious injury. The internal bleeding had been minor—thank God. Mark Baker's body had taken the brunt of the explosion.

Thursday morning, Quinn left her because he had to—he had to go to his own appointment with Barroso. But Barbara insisted he eat breakfast with her first. She had something she wanted to tell him. He agreed and met her in the cafeteria at the hospital.

Hannah's mother ate a muffin while Quinn wolfed down scrambled eggs and hash browns and tried not to look at his watch too many times. He wanted everything done so he could return to Hannah.

Barbara put her napkin beside her plate and made a sound of exasperation. "What is your problem, Quinn? Hannah will be fine by herself long enough for you to eat and see your doctor. Can't you relax for two minutes?"

He wrapped his hands around his mug and stared at the coffee. "No. I guess I can't." He raised his eyes. "Not until I know she's going to be all right."

"Haven't the doctors already told you she would be?"

He nodded.

"So?"

"You said it yourself," he answered. She frowned and he continued. "There are no guarantees...remember? They may say she's going to recover, but I'll worry until I see proof of that myself."

She shook her head. "You take the cake, Quinn, I swear...."

He put his elbows on the table. "I love her too damn much, Barbara."

"I know," she said softly. "And that's why you need to do something about it." She waited until his eyes met hers again. "If you don't, you'll regret it the rest of your life."

He nodded but said nothing else. They were walking out of the dining room and heading for the elevators when Barbara gave him her news. "After Hannah's back on her feet, I'm moving in with Lindsey. I think it's time I give Hannah some space." She grimaced. "And frankly, I need a bit of my own as well. My daughter is not the easiest person in the world to live with, you know."

Quinn grinned. "I'm well aware of that fact. She likes things done her way."

"She does," Barbara agreed. "But so do I, so I

understand. Lindsey's much more easygoing, though. Nothing much bothers her. Besides that, we're two little old ladies—we see the world the same way. It's nice to be around someone like that.''

They reached the elevators and stopped, Barbara looking up at Quinn, her expression becoming sharp after she wished him luck at Barroso's office.

"So Hannah's going to be alone once she recovers," she said pointedly.

"I understand."

"All by herself in that house."

He nodded.

"Well? Are you going to do something about that or not?"

"I don't know," he answered honestly. "I just don't know."

She stared at him a little longer, then she shook her head and walked away stiffly. He was stupid beyond belief, her reproachful back seemed to say.

He turned around and headed to the medical offices next door that housed Barroso's office. He would have liked to confide in Barbara, but he wasn't sure he knew how to express what was happening. All he knew for certain was that deep down, Quinn sensed a change taking place. It had begun when he'd realized what Bobby had done. And it had grown stronger as he'd sat by Hannah's side.

After a treadmill test and countless X rays, Barroso came into the examining room where Quinn waited. The doctor wore his usual white coat, which was starched and spotless, but beneath it the collar of a blue shirt peeked out, a silk tie knotted carefully at the neck. He was frowning as he looked at the clipboard in his hands.

Quinn attempted to lighten the moment. "You look awfully sharp today. That nurse on the eighth floor finally snag you?"

"Which one, amigo? The blonde or the redhead? Be specific."

"Either would be fine."

"You're right about that." The doctor grinned, but then his expression slowly faded. He tapped the reports he held. "What isn't so fine are these...."

Quinn tensed, every muscle in his body going tight with sudden anxiety. "Tell me about them."

"I don't think I have to do that." Barroso propped his foot on the chair next to the examining table and stared at Quinn with troubled brown eyes. "I think you already know what they say."

In the silence that followed, Quinn heard a door open and close. The finality of the sound seemed fitting. He sighed and looked out the window, then when his heart had settled down, he spoke, his gaze still outside. "You're not going to release me, are you?"

Barroso's answer surprised him. "I think I need to leave that decision up to you."

Quinn stared at the doctor. "What the hell does that mean?"

"It means you have not recovered as you should have. The leg is still not strong enough because we had to take out so much muscle. The strength, it isn't there. But there are ways around this."

"Such as?"

"Operations, therapy, drugs… You name it, we can do it."

"Will it fix the problem?"

"I don't know. It's impossible to say at this point."

"I thought doctors were supposed to know everything."

"That, my friend, is a myth, because only you can know the answer to this." He looked at Quinn with speculation. "The decision is in your hands. I can reinstate you and begin the process, but you need to decide what you really want."

All at once, Quinn realized he didn't have to think about the choice. He'd known before he'd walked into the doctor's office. Having the question put to him this way only reinforced his resolution.

Standing up, he reached for his clothes and began to dress. When he finished, he told the doctor exactly what he wanted.

What he *really* wanted.

HANNAH LEFT THE HOSPITAL a week after the explosion. Her chest still hurt and every breath brought pain. Sitting on the porch of her bungalow the following Sunday, she let the weak November sun chase the cold from her body as she tried to blank her mind. But her thoughts were a jumble, just as they had been since she'd begun to recover.

"We're leaving now." Barbara stuck her head out the back door and looked at Hannah. "Will you be okay for a little while?"

"I'll be fine," Hannah repeated for what seemed like the fifteenth time. It was bingo night, and for days a big discussion had taken place over whether Barbara and Lindsey should go or not. "You two go on—just enjoy yourselves and don't worry about me. Stop by and check out your new apartment, too. See if it's ready yet."

"Are you trying to get rid of me?"

Hannah rolled her eyes. "Ma, c'mon. I wasn't trying to say anything like that—"

Lindsey tugged at her friend's sweater. "For goodness' sake, Barb, leave the poor girl alone. She wants some peace and quiet. Who wouldn't after what she's been through?"

Hannah smiled her gratefulness at Lindsey. She *was* ready for some time by herself, but it wouldn't be peaceful or quiet, she was sure. She had too much thinking to do for that to be the case.

Barbara hesitated a moment more, then she nodded. "All right...but you call us if you need us. We can come right back. And we *will* stop by the complex before bingo...."

Hannah waved the women away. When they left the house, she sighed in relief. Then she closed her eyes, her thoughts immediately jumping to Quinn.

She'd seen Quinn every day following the explosion. At the hospital he'd sat quietly and read as she'd slept. After she'd come home, he'd shown up at different times with small gifts—magazines, flowers, things like that. She had the unexplained feeling he was marking time, but that didn't seem to matter. The pull of his personality was as strong as ever, the feelings between them undiminished by anything that had happened. She needed him as much as she needed the air she breathed.

She cursed herself and then him. Why did it have to be this way? Why couldn't she fall in love with someone else? Was Quinn the only man she'd ever feel this passionately about? She'd had a vision of the life she'd wanted for so long that it seemed as if it was a part of her, like an arm or a leg. Could she sever that hope and be satisfied with the love he gave her?

A sudden shooting pain took her mind away from her questions, her aching ribs reminding her of the accident in a way she couldn't ignore. Wincing as she shifted in her seat, she wished she could curse Bobby as Quinn had. He'd told her of the aftermath, of the bomb, of his fight with Bobby. She understood Quinn's anger, but that was a male way of dealing with things. Her own reaction had contained anger, of course, but it'd been much more complicated than Quinn's. A mixture of grief and disappointment, confusion and betrayal continued to haunt her.

Nothing was ever simple.

A thought that brought her straight back to the relationship between her and Quinn.

He wasn't the same man he'd been when he'd walked into that day-care center, and the events of the recent past had highlighted that fact. When she'd first seen him in St. Martin she'd thought him harder, but now she knew for sure. He *was* tougher, edgier somehow, as if everything that had happened to them both had carved him into a sharper relief. She wondered about the changes and what they meant to the two of them.

Her musings were interrupted by a car pulling into the driveway.

A few seconds later, Quinn rounded the corner of the house. He stood motionless in the sunshine, his dark eyes capturing Hannah's with a look that sent her heart into overtime. He wore jeans and a T-shirt, and he'd gotten a haircut. Everything about him reinforced her assessment of him only moments before.

Hannah stared at him. "Hi," she finally said.

"Hello yourself." He sat down on the first porch step.

They sat in silence, Hannah wondering what she should say next. It was strange to feel so awkward around Quinn. He saved her by speaking first.

"I got a call from Lena. She wanted you to know Pinkley signed a confession after you left. He owned up to everything, except New Orleans, of course. He said it was a love letter—to you."

Hannah shivered, the serial bomber's cold and empty eyes a memory she'd rather not keep.

"I got a call from Boston Bomb, too."

"About Mark?"

Quinn nodded slowly, his eyes on the magnolia tree in her front yard. "His brother's last name wasn't Baker because he was Mark's stepbrother. One of the team members who'd been on leave came back and he remembered. He called me and confirmed Mark's story."

The way his voice trailed off, Hannah knew there was more. She waited.

After a bit, he turned his head and looked at her. "Mark's family wouldn't have anything to do with him after he became an EXIT member. There was a lot of money—his father and mother owned a very successful business—and they had always expected the kids to join the firm. When the first son ignored their wishes and got killed, they were devastated. Apparently he was Mark's hero, though. Mark followed in his footsteps and they disowned him completely.''

Hannah's throat closed, a lump forming as she remembered Mark's bleak home. ''How awful.''

He picked up an errant leaf from the porch step and held it by the stem. ''I spoke with Janie last night, too. It's been pretty bad for them, especially the kids. The television crews are still outside their door.''

Hannah thought of the beautiful family Bobby had left behind. ''You didn't tell her what he said, did you?''

Quinn shook his head. ''That would serve no purpose. And Bobby didn't do what he did because of anything she said. He has demons that none of us knew about, including her.''

They sat in silence, each lost in the past few months and everything that had happened between them. A deep ache rose in Hannah's heart for all they'd been through…and all that had been sacrificed, willingly and otherwise. The image of two tiny caskets came into her mind. Quinn spoke and banished them.

"I think we need to talk."

She looked at his face. In the past, that had been Hannah's line. Quinn's response had always been a back rub, or a kiss, or a direct assault on her body. Anything to distract her. His words set off an earthquake inside her.

"All right," she said somewhat tentatively. "Let's talk."

He waited such a long time to begin she finally decided he'd changed his mind. Then he raised his eyes, and the revelation in his gaze reached deep inside her. As always, her body responded...but this time so did her heart.

"I've been wrong about something that's very, very important."

She held her breath and he spoke again.

"But I've also been right," he said. "We need to figure out which is which...."

Hannah blamed her jumping pulse on her confusion. "I'm not sure I understand."

He reached over and took her fingers in his. The desire that instantly flowed between them was hot and quick. It infused her with the kind of energy she'd been missing since their breakup.

"I love you," he started.

"Is that the right part or the wrong part?" Her voice was teasing, but she truly wondered.

He smiled and her heart sped up even more. "That's some of the right part."

"Now I'm really confused."

"So was I," he said. "But not anymore. Not after everything that happened."

He turned her hand over and gently caressed the inside of her palm. "I love you," he repeated quietly. "And that's very right. But the way I handled our relationship wasn't." He gripped her hand suddenly, his gaze piercing hers. "I never wanted children because I was afraid we might not come home one night. I couldn't bear the thought of you raising our family alone or of me doing the same. Or worse, both of us going at once. Who would take care of them? Who would be responsible for them?" He paused. "The idea of something like that happening still scares the shit out of me, but I've come to understand we can't always dictate the perfect time and place. Our life isn't totally under our control. Sometimes decisions are made *for* us, instead of by us." His expression shifted in a way she couldn't read. "And maybe, in the long run, that's the way it ought to be...."

Hannah spoke softly. "Well, believe it or not, I understand your feelings now much better than I did before. When I saw Mark die..." She shivered, her

her gaze going someplace she couldn't forget before it returned to Quinn. "One minute he was standing there and the next, he was gone. It made me see how fragile life really is. You can't take it for granted. Not one single day."

"Does that mean you don't want children anymore?"

She looked him square in the eye, her decision coming swiftly. "No. It means I want them even more. But not while I'm doing what I do now." She took a deep breath. "I'm going to ask for a transfer, Quinn. I want a desk job. I've never had the instincts you have and it's time for me to focus on what I do best—analysis. I'm getting out of the field."

"So am I."

Her mouth fell open. "Quinn! You're the best! You can't leave—"

He held up his hand. "I met with Barroso while you were in the hospital. He said he could reinstate me, but he'd have a lot more work to do on my leg, maybe even another surgery. He said it was up to me."

"Oh, Quinn…" Hannah felt her heart break for the man beside her. She knew how much his job meant to him, how much a part of him it had become. "I'm so sorry."

"There's no reason for that. I'd already made the decision to leave before I even went into his office."

Her heart thudded. "Why?"

"I've been offered a teaching position at EU-BDC. They needed people and Bill Ford asked if I'd let him recommend me. I said yes and so did they."

"How wonderful, Quinn! I'm thrilled for you. That's such an honor...." She'd attended classes at the Explosives Unit—Bomb Data Center. Run by the FBI, the federal agency supported bomb techs all over the world. The facility was incredible, the trainers exceptional.

"That's not why I made the decision I did, Hannah." Moving to where she sat, he kneeled down, putting his arms around her. "I made it because you are the most important thing in my life and I want to put you first. Without you beside me, nothing has meaning."

"Oh, Quinn..." The strength of his embrace and all it meant warmed her instantly. And deeply. She felt herself melt.

"They need other techs, too. They'd hire you in a minute. For analysis or anything else you wanted to do."

She pulled back in surprise, her shock giving way to delight. "Do you really think so?"

"I know so. In fact, I told Bill we were a package deal. All or nothing."

Hannah shook her head in amazement. He'd read

her mind again, known what she wanted even before she knew herself.

He spoke quietly, his voice alone was enough to send a shiver up her back. "Will you marry me, Hannah Crosby? Will you be my wife and have my children?"

Hannah gripped his arms, her heart in her throat, every dream she'd ever had suddenly within reach. "Yes, I will," she said, her eyes shining. "I'd like nothing better than to be your wife. And as far as the children thing goes...do you think we could start on that this evening?"

He grinned and brought her closer, the thrill of his body against her own as new and exciting as the first time they'd touched. When he answered her question, his gaze was tender but just a little bit wicked, too.

"Why wait that long?" His eyes gleamed as he asked. "I say we get started right now. There's no time like the present."

"You're absolutely right," she answered. "So quit wasting time and carry me inside...."

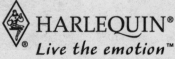

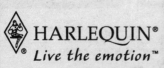

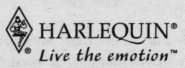